Glasshouse

Morwenna Blackwood

Also by the author:

The (D)Evolution of Us

DARK
STROKE

www.darkstroke.com

Discover us online:
www.darkstroke.com

Find us on instagram:
www.instagram.com/darkstrokebooks

Include **#darkstroke** in a photo of yourself
holding this book on Instagram and
something nice will happen.

To the one-in-four.

About the Author

When Morwenna Blackwood was six years old, she got told off for filling a school exercise book with an endless story when she should have been listening to the teacher/eating her tea/colouring with her friends. The story was about a frog. It never did end; and Morwenna never looked back.

Born and raised in Devon, Morwenna suffered from severe OCD and depression, and spent her childhood and teens in libraries. She travelled about for a decade before returning to Devon. She now has an MA in Creative Writing from the University of Exeter, and lives with her husband, son and three cats in a cottage that Bilbo Baggins would be proud of. When she is not writing, she works for an animal rescue charity, or can be found down by the sea.

She often thinks about that frog.

Acknowledgements

Firstly, I'd like to thank Phil and K for their unending love and patience, and for making the process of writing novels possible!

Sincere thanks to Dad; to KJB; and to Lee Dickinson – again - for his superb editing. Also to Laurence and Steph, and the darkstroke community for their support, encouragement, dedication, advice and their sense of humour – I'm extremely happy and proud to be a part of this!

As ever, thanks to my great friend-since-school and fellow author, Roland, for helping me keep the writing faith; and to Karen for so, so many things over the years, including for getting me out in the first place!

Finally, thanks to the NHS – now more than ever.

Glasshouse

Prologue

Spring 1999
Julia

I hit the brakes. There's a couple crying on the pelican crossing outside the hospital. I miss them by inches. The man holds the woman back when she starts screaming at me; maybe he's seen the state of my face. Once he's pulled her clear of the road, I stamp on the accelerator, and abandon the car in the ambulance bay.

A few of the smokers outside the main entrance scowl and shout things at me, but I barely register them and push my way through to the big plan of the hospital that takes up most of the wall in the reception area. I scan the list of wards for the one Sasha told me Elizabeth is in, locate it on the map, and run down the corridor.

I'm not worried that I'm causing a scene – I figure that people will think I'm a desperate relative trying to make it to a dying loved one in time – so I don't stop running until I reach the ward. I stand in the crowd of people around the nurses' station and look for her name on the board; I can't believe my luck: she's tucked away in the far corner, with the curtains closed around her bed. Hiding in plain sight, I rush down the ward to her bed, check there are no doctors in with her, and slip behind the curtain.

Elizabeth looks tiny in the bed, like a child. I note that her hair is dark. She is lying down, and I can't see her face. There are tubes and wires attached to her, and a monitor is beeping steadily. My hands are clenched, and I'm suddenly aware that they're sweating. I approach the head of the bed. Elizabeth's eyes are closed, and she is breathing regularly. I presume she's asleep – if she was in an induced coma, she'd be in a more secure ward, surely.

I stand there, running my fingers across my damp palms, looking at her. She's pretty – that's evident even under the oxygen mask. I consider pulling all the plugs out of the wall but check myself – the monitors will be alarmed. I try to remember all the episodes of *Casualty* I've seen. I sit down in the inevitable uncomfortably upright chair next to her bed, absentmindedly moving the spare cushion that was on the seat, onto the moving table thing that holds a dry plastic tumbler, and a jug of water. I sit like this for some minutes before the obvious occurs to me. This whole situation started with her. If Erazmus hadn't met her, I would not have lost my baby. I stand, pick up the cushion, pull the mask from her face, try to commit her features to memory, and using both hands, I press the cushion into her face.

Autumn 1998
Lizzie

The patterns, the symbolism – it's like a code that I'm beginning to decipher. I sketch the moments that seem important, in the hopes that one day I'll understand it all.

Everything became real- or at least documented - years ago. I was in my mid-teens, making my lonely way to the doctor, wearing ripped jeans and an old blazer of my mum's that she used to wear to work. I was crying, as usual. It was raining heavily and all the colours in the world had been mushed into a green, brown and grey slop. I was soaked by the time I arrived at the surgery, so my tears were disguised, although my eyes must have been puffy and red. I'd cultivated a habit of going to the doctor in recent months, with aches and pains, insomnia, dizziness. This time I didn't know whether the doctor was the right person to tell, but I needed to tell someone. I thought I was going mad. I couldn't stop crying, and I had no reason to cry. I felt alienated from the world – my family, the lyrics in songs, my books, the things my friends were talking about, the things I was learning at school. I was pretty sure I was going to die before I reached twenty, and I was pretty sure how. The worst thing was that my mind was jumping around, and I was kind of remembering things that couldn't possibly have happened. I couldn't even describe it properly. I thought I might have schizophrenia. I was *hoping* I had schizophrenia.

I didn't have schizophrenia, and I was gutted. If I'd had a proper illness, that would have been the end of it. But the doctor just diagnosed me with clinical depression, gave me a prescription for Prozac, and referred me to a psychiatrist. I went to my appointment, hoping the man in the white coat would lock me up, but he'd been in a tweed suit, not a white coat, and hadn't looked that much older than me. He said I'd had a flashback of being sexually abused, and that had affected me profoundly, but if I kept taking my medication, and focused on my studies instead of my 'intrusive thoughts', there was no reason why I wouldn't feel better and be able to live a full life. But I didn't feel any better.

The years passed and I still didn't feel any better, so I stopped taking my tablets and saved them up instead. The night before my twentieth birthday, I went down by the river and forced myself to drink a pint of vodka while swallowing as many of my tablets as I could. Then I jumped off the bridge. I remember lots of screaming and shouting, and when the red-and-white-striped life ring splashed onto the water near me, I turned my face away and waited to drown. But the river carried me downstream only as far as the weir, where I got stuck and someone dragged me out. I ended up in A&E after that and was later transferred to a residential psychiatric care home in Bishopsham, called The Stables.

The Stables is an extensive building with a well-tended garden. There's a bay window at the front near the porch, which is framed by a heavy wisteria that's a purple fog in summer and a labyrinth of tendrils in winter. A path meanders from the steeply sloping drive up to the porch, through the cottage garden – a tangle of rambling dog roses, forget-me-nots and honeysuckle: plants that creep and spread. In front of the porch is a kidney-shaped pond which is home to several ornamental carp and is covered by a strong mesh. Initially, I thought that the mesh was to protect the fish from the resident cat; later it became apparent that the true purpose of the mesh was to stop the resident humans attempting to drown themselves. When I get particularly stressed, I come and sit out here under the wisteria, and smoke a thousand cigarettes.

There are eight of us patients, or inmates, or whatever our official moniker is, and about a dozen staff of varying rank, who work seemingly random shifts in order to keep everything and everyone safe, twenty-four hours a day, 365 days a year. In addition to our bedrooms, there's a massive sitting room with battered old sofas and too many floral cushions, and a fireplace that's no longer in use. I suppose having a roaring real fire in a room full of schizophrenics, pyromaniacs and self-harmers isn't a good idea. However, everyone smokes, and no matter how many fragrant roses are cut and brought in from the garden, or how wide the windows are opened, the room still stinks of cigarettes. When I accidentally knock the pictures while I'm dusting them, you can see that the wallpaper was originally white behind its floral pattern, not cream.

I get up, shower, do my chore for the day, then sit down in the front room with a coffee and a rollie, like I need a rest. To be honest, though, I do need a rest. I'm in a constant state of exhaustion; my head feels so heavy that some days it's a struggle to even lift it. I ask myself daily why I don't just do the world a favour and kill myself. The utter tedium of thinking the same thing over and over again has me banging my head against walls; I realise this act is madness in itself, as that's become tedious too. Also, they've threatened me with a secure unit if I don't stop. Some days I can't understand why I've been sent to The Stables – it's so fucking stressful. They told me it was for respite, and yet I have to do a daily chore, and eat with the others and get up and get dressed every day. All I want to do is stay in bed, but if I stay in bed, I can't sleep and I ache, and I realise that my shoulders are hunched up to my ears and I'm clenching my jaw. Sometimes it clicks when I'm eating. Seriously, is there no escape? Yes, there is, but now I'm at The Stables, the only things I've slashed are my options.

Phoenix ('just call me 'Phee''), the new psychologist I've been assigned to, explains to me when I've calmed down after an outburst in our session one evening, that the chores are designed to keep us living 'normally', and that 'respite' doesn't mean that we'll be waited on while we float around doing as we please.

The Stables is, essentially, a rehabilitation centre – I have to work to recover. This is a revelation to me. For years I've felt side-lined because mental illness isn't socially accepted in the way that physical illness is; now I'm realising that you can't have it both ways. If you tear a ligament and your wrist hurts and doesn't function properly, you have to do physiotherapy in addition to taking medication. Here – to get my brain to heal – as well as pumping myself full of drugs, I have to get on with the necessities of being alive, which means getting up, interacting with people, eating and cleaning things. Hence the 'chores' system.

The 'chores' are on a rolling rota, and are one of: 1) cleaning the dining room, 2) cleaning the front room, 3) cleaning the bathrooms, 4) cleaning the laundry room, 5) garden chores, 6) shopping, 7) day off – the day I live for!; and then there's chore 8) the dreaded cooking chore. The whole thing is bad enough in itself, but it annoys me that there are more chores than days in the week. Perhaps this is another test.

Cooking day brings out the best and worst in people. Lydia has been used to cooking what I think of as extravagant meals for her fiancé. They'd been planning to open a restaurant. By extravagant, I mean using stuff like fresh herbs and root ginger and a pestle and mortar. I'd never even seen ginger before I came to The Stables. I thought it was a powder. When it's Lydia's turn to cook, everyone gets excited because we know we'll be getting a meal that would pass at The Ritz; Lydia loves it because it's so easy for her, and it makes her happy. She seems to not see her 'shadows' so much when she's cooking, either – at least she never shows that she does. The person behind the illness is evident and in control – Dr Jekyll winning over Mr Hyde for a moment.

By contrast, there is – or, rather, was – Jessica. Jessica is – was, whatever – an anorexic. When she'd arrived at The Stables, I'd been outside by the pond, smoking. A big, black vehicle had pulled up, and five people had got out. Four of them had formed a ring around the fifth, as if they were petals around an anther. Or flies on a carcass. The one in the middle was short and very slight, and someone had covered her – I presumed it was a girl – head with a towel. The strange cluster of people had scurried from the car through the mizzle hanging in the air, and in through the opened front door. We hadn't seen Jessica properly until the next day. She turned out to be bird-like, and the whole time she was here we never saw her eat or drink. She'd stayed in her room as much as they'd let her. Suddenly a week had gone by, and it was her cook day.

She hadn't even been able to open the fridge. She'd been screaming and crying in the kitchen, and those of us who'd run to see what was going on had been ushered away. I think every member of staff on duty had been in the kitchen in the end; two of them had been restraining her as she writhed like a captured animal. Bonnie, one of the support staff, had been trying to get her to open the fridge – that was all; if you could say that about anything at The Stables. Eventually, the managers, Heather and Dunstan, had escorted Jessica to her room and given her a sedative; Bonnie had made the rest of us beans on toast for tea. Lydia and I had been surprised that they'd insisted on Jessica doing another cook day, but Heather had put her foot down – everyone struggled with something, and no one else got a free pass, she'd said. But it had been even worse than the first time – Jessica had picked up a peeling knife and sliced her wrist open. Her blood had spurted out over everything and everyone. An ambulance had arrived, and that was the last we'd seen of Jessica. Maybe she'd gone to an AAU. Maybe she'd gone to the secure unit in Torquay. Maybe she'd gone to the morgue. Bonnie and the team had thought they'd done a thorough clean-up, but I can still see some flecks of red in the grouting.

AAU is short for Acute Admissions Unit. It's basically a safe-holding area they put you in while they work out what to do with you. I've only ever been in two – one just for a night, the second time for a month. The first time I was admitted, I'd been living in what they called a 'halfway house': a semi-supported place to live for those who were nearly ready to be let back into the community, and for people like me, who,

9

though they needed support and needed to be out of the situation they were in, weren't unstable enough to warrant locking up. It was a normal house in the middle of a normal terrace in a normal street in the small seaside town of Swansburne. I don't believe that half of the people living on the street knew what number nine was used for – I think most of them thought it was a student let or something. There were six of us residents, and the house was staffed only during the day. This made me laugh because if anything was going to happen, it was going to happen after dark. I was in recovery and was doing well – until I met one of my fellow residents, Dom, on the beach one afternoon. There really wasn't much to do, without a job, and being all but estranged from my family and friends, so I spent hours – sometimes whole days – walking along the shoreline and the coastal paths. As a child, I'd collected shells washed up on the sand and made mosaics from them, and I found myself doing this again; but I'd discovered something new – smooth, almost speckled, emerald gems, and I began to collect them. I was doing this one day, walking along the shore, scanning the sand, when I saw Dom, sitting as near to the surf as he could on dry sand, skimming pebbles, and smoking a rollie. Dom was tall and wiry; his hair was naturally very dark, but he dyed it red. His eyes were as grey as the sky and the sea. I sat down next to him – as near as I could without shaking – and waited for him to realise I was there. When he did, he just smiled and passed me his tobacco pouch. I had to put down the handful of smooth green stones I was clutching to take it from him, and he said, "Oh. Sea glass. My mum used to collect that." Sea glass. It had a name. More importantly, Dom and I had a connection.

Dom was schizophrenic – also in recovery, also doing well; and also gorgeous – although he did have a slight paunch due to the meds he was on. He was twenty-six and had been in art college until his breakdown. He'd shown me photos of the walls of his room in the studio basement flat he had lived in before he'd been packed off to hospital – he'd sprayed them, graffiti-style, and they were kaleidoscopic. His landlord hadn't been impressed, apparently, and had tried to evict him, but Dom had claimed squatters' rights. The police got involved, and his section shortly followed. But he was an artist, like me – of course I fell in love with him.

There was a problem, though: he was in a relationship with another girl in the house, who also had schizophrenia. Her name was Rebecca, and as I came to love Dom, I came to hate her. They 'understood' each other, because of what they'd 'been through' in a way that no one else could, apparently. That's what Rebecca – never 'Becky' or 'Bex', which grated on me even more – told everyone. She said it all the time, and the way she said it, it was like no one else's diagnosis counted; like schizophrenia was the pinnacle of mental illness, and everyone else was just whingeing and needed to get a grip. Dom said very little to anyone – about their relationship, about his illness, about anything, really. Except his art. If you showed an interest in it, he'd talk forever. It was like an obsession, and I could never understand why Rebecca didn't seem to think it was important. I'd have had one of his designs tattooed on me if I'd been her – I would have been proud to go out with him because he was an artist, not just because he had the same diagnosis – I'd have cut one into my arm. The thing I used to hate the most, though, and what eventually drove me to distraction, was when they used to sit in the TV room. It was a small room, with a grey two-seater sofa and two matching, uncomfortable armchairs. A bloke called Marcus was always in the chair closest to the TV – he sat there all day, twiddling his dreadlocks, only getting up when his tea had gone cold, to make himself a new one that he let get cold. He drank lemongrass tea. He said it was a form of self-medication and that he was trying to improve his memory. He said he was trying to get back the things he had forgotten. He said it wasn't fair, having to buy expensive products like that when you're on DLA.

I tried herbal teas too, for a bit, for the same reason. Sometimes, when my benefits had gone in, I'd catch the train to Totnes and go to the 'hippy' shop to spend an hour in their floatation tank. It was supposedly good for recovering suppressed memories. I knew there were other things stored in my head somewhere, because this is where the flashbacks had come from. For whatever reason, I just couldn't access them. It was like I had a blank, white space in my head; like a dust sheet thrown over all the stuff in a loft. I wanted to see the horrors that lurked beneath. I wanted to know who I really was. It felt important.

Meanwhile, Dom and Rebecca used to sit there in the TV room on the two-seater sofa, holding hands. Simple, inoffensive, undemonstrative, unbearable. One dank afternoon, after having sat there trying to concentrate on *Quincy,* I conceded. I stormed up to my room and didn't come out. I stopped eating. I just sat in my armchair, staring out of the window, listening to Radiohead and drinking lemongrass tea. Two whole days passed before one of the support staff – Claudia, I think her name was, she was mainly red lipstick and hairspray – banged on my door and asked me what was wrong. I told her I was fine. She made me a cup of tea, left it outside my door, and gently advised me to come out with her for a coffee and a cake the next morning, and get whatever was bothering me off my chest. But the next morning, I'd crossed that line in my head – by which I mean the blackness in my soul had permeated everything, literally everything. I didn't get out of bed that day. I stayed face down under the quilt, like a cat hiding its face so no one can see it, as the chaos built behind me. There were knocks of varying loudness on my door, voices shouting and murmuring, cajoling, pleading, demanding, and eventually, threatening. Someone got the skeleton key and unlocked my door. I didn't respond to anything they did, and I kept my face hidden, even though I was uncomfortable. Then everyone went away. Hours passed. Eventually I heard a voice I didn't recognise, and something made me turn my head in its direction. A kind man in a shabby suit and an anorak suggested I should go to hospital. He helped me to the loo, where I relieved myself and splashed water on my face, letting it run over my wrists. Intuitively, I knew I should try to clear my head, but I simultaneously hoped that this was it – the point at which I went under. Then I would be free. Finally, I was guided out of the front door and down the steps, and a nurse and the man in the anorak bundled me into the back of a car. Claudia was there, and I was surprised at the level of sadness in her expression. Dom had the grace, and Rebecca had the gall, to stand at the top of the steps and watch as I was taken away.

The journey is a blur, but I remember a beige building, with beige paint and beige furniture, several floors up; a grille in the door of my room, so that the staff could check on me every fifteen minutes; a bed and a table that were fixed to the floor. No sharps, no belts, no laces, no pills were allowed, so they searched me, and my bag. It was chaos, it was hot, it was loud. There were people milling about everywhere; the door to a toilet was open and loo roll had spilled out across the floor; I struggled to differentiate patient from healthcare professional. A snooker match was showing on the TV, and one inmate was swearing blind he was Ronnie O'Sullivan, and he'd played the game he was watching days ago, even though it was live. People were tapping at computers in an office shielded by fortified glass. There was so much noise – how was this good for people who were suffering with psychiatric disorders? I was interviewed, and was made to feel like I was wasting everyone's time – the nurses were looking at me like I had no right to be there. Eventually, I was given a sedative, and was glad when they shut me in a beige room; but I'd heard them talking when they thought I couldn't hear. They were expressing their concern – my room was on the male wing because all the beds on the female side were occupied, and the angry woman who'd interviewed me exclaimed, "Who the hell brought her here, anyway?! Swansburne CMHT? What are they playing at?!" In spite of this – probably due to the sedative – I slept well, and in the morning I was moved to The Bungalow – a kind of self-contained flat in the hospital grounds. I never saw Rebecca again, and it would be years before I re-encountered Dom.

My second experience of an AAU couldn't have been

more different, maybe because it was several years later, maybe because of a change in government policy. It was after I'd ODd and jumped off the bridge. It was where I first met Dr Whittle. I'd been transferred to the unit after spending a day and a night in A&E – all I recall of that time is sitting on the edge of a hospital bed, swinging my legs, wondering where my shoes had gone, with the overall impression that everyone was very nice.

My memory of my first day in the psych unit is also blurry, and the only thing that really sticks in my mind is the plastic mugs. We were sitting in the canteen; me, Mum and Dad, and my brother, Ant. No one knew what to say, and I was high on sedatives and meds, so we all commented on the rainbow of plastic mugs from which we were drinking a tepid, light-brown substance that was masquerading as tea. The tea was already made, and you got it by turning a tap on an urn – apparently, we couldn't be trusted with kettles and spoons. It was quiet. There were a few people walking around, and I noted that the staff greeted the patients by name as they passed. There was an office where people in smart clothes were typing, but the door was wedged ajar. Two blokes were playing pool in a games room, *Toy Story* was on in the TV room, and everyone else was in the garden, smoking. The toilets were clean and were off the main walkway. It seemed peaceful and well-organised. A clinical home from home.

In the middle of the morning of my second day, I was introduced to Dr Whittle. I was being assessed again, in an office that I hadn't noticed before, the door of this one being firmly closed. Seven of us, myself included, sat politely on chairs that looked like they belonged in a cafe: three members of ward staff, a secretary, Phee – my psychologist, who wore earrings so heavy and dangly I worried her earlobes would tear – and, I ascertained from the photo ID hanging around his neck, Dr Erazmus Whittle, Consultant Psychiatrist. He smiled, then redundantly introduced himself. My breath caught in my throat. Dr Whittle was in his forties, I guessed. He was tall and wiry, with thick, dark hair and

14

bright blue eyes which locked onto my own and barely shifted from them for the duration of the meeting. This panel, or whatever they were, had obviously read my file, because I wasn't asked to recount my history: they were only concerned with how I was feeling then. I had to fill in the usual questionnaire – in the last four weeks, did I agree strongly, agree, neither agree nor disagree, disagree or disagree strongly with statements like, 'I have wanted to harm myself' and 'I have felt completely without hope' – and then I had a meds review. As I wasn't sleeping, I was prescribed zopiclone; and as I had long-standing and persistent depression, as well as obsessive tendencies, Dr Whittle suggested I add lithium and risperidone to the sertraline and pregabalin that I was already taking. Lithium scared me – it was well-known, and hard-core – Nirvana had written a song about it. It meant regular blood tests, and I was scared of needles. Before my incarceration, I'd been 'self-medicating' whenever I could with whatever alcohol and drugs I could get my hands on, because my prescription drugs didn't allow me to escape. Obviously, this had stopped, but I wondered how much damage I'd already done. And how I would cope, permanently sober? Did I even stand a chance? And the alcohol and drugs – that was a separate issue, wasn't it? Or part of the same issue? Or not an issue at all? They said I needed respite, and I'd be at the unit for a while.

'A while' turned out to be a month, during which time they'd found me a place in a residential care home in Bishopsham – The Stables. I didn't see Dr Whittle for the whole of the rest of the time I was there in hospital, and I couldn't understand why. I caught myself looking out for him whenever I passed the office, and berated myself for my need to have something to obsess about. So I just got up, showered, drank tea from plastic mugs, read, mooched, had a bit of lunch, went on the exercise bike, had tea, and then my folks would visit me in the evening. They came up every single evening I was there.

Erazmus

I return to the hospital car park to find that someone has parked their forest-green Jaguar in my allocated space. All the other staff spaces are taken, so I have to park in the visitors' area, which means I have to pay £2.50 right now and come back to pay some more in two hours. Jags smack of jumped-up idiots and middle-management. I wonder which department is having its budget cut next. It had better not be mine. I feel my body tense, so I have a go at the breathing exercises I'm forever recommending to my patients. Okay, they have a point – it's not easy, or particularly effective, because my mind has raced on, and I am dreading the inevitable pore-saturating odour that is going to accost me when I enter the building. Hospital lunches. It's the same smell at all hospitals up and down the country at midday. I pause before entering the building through the automatic doors, and take my last breath of clean air. Stepping inside, I smile at the girls on reception. I say 'girls', but they're probably in their late twenties. The concept of age has altered significantly for me since I reached forty.

It amuses me that each hospital is given a personality. No one is fooled – these are not homely, friendly places. In fact, to my mind, the fact that they cover the walls with pictures by local artists, and commission some well-meaning but talentless person to paint a mural in the kids' corner, actually makes it worse. I'd rather we were up-front and honest about it and had pictures of drips, cannulas, scalpels, ventilators ... maybe an art student from the college could make a sculpture out of mis-prescribed antibiotics and unused antipsychotics. The architect who designed this hospital was an arachnophile – he based his design on a spider's web. Reception is the spider, sitting in the middle of its creation, waiting for unsuspecting visitors; corridors to the different departments shoot off from this central area, with rooms at regular places along them; the department hub being at the end of each corridor, as the point of contact where the web is attached to the objects that support it. There are two identical storeys, and I mount the stairs to the mezzanine, only just avoiding the ever-present 'caution – wet floor' sign. The floor is no longer wet, but it had been when the cleaner left at 8.30 a.m.; nobody seems to be capable of putting the sign back in the cleaner's storeroom but me. I am aware that I am letting trivial things annoy me, and I catch myself automatically mentally blaming my wife, Julia, which is also ridiculous. I am responsible for my life. I know I need to make a change, and I will. But right now I am at work, and I need to focus on my patients.

To access my office and the treatment rooms, you have to walk through the departmental waiting room. I say 'departmental waiting room' – it's essentially a corridor with chairs pushed up against the walls, and two royal blue screens placed across so that you can't see who is sitting on the chairs as you enter the building. They only do this for the psych department, as if being there is something to be ashamed of. Squeezing through this crack to enter my workplace always makes me feel as though I'm going potholing, even though this part of the hospital is called The Meadows. There isn't even a fish tank – there isn't room – just a low table bearing its standard offering of tissues and out-of-date magazines. There are four chairs on each side, and to get to the receptionists' hatch and into the clinical area, you have to walk up the middle of them. I wonder how this affects us all, subconsciously. Also, it means you can see who is waiting for you, or one of the other members of the team; who is distressed; who is new. The patients follow you with their eyes, wondering what will happen, wondering if today is the day they'll be 'cured'. My team and I are good – but we're not miracle workers: there is no cure, only recovery. There's only one receptionist on in The Meadows at this time, because of staff lunch breaks – a pretty little thing who wears too much make-up and calls herself Candy. Her name is actually Charlotte, but she is sweet, so her chosen moniker is fitting. She grins and waves at me as she takes a phone call. I wonder if she'll be offended if I ask her to pop out and get me a sandwich. I haven't had a lunch break since I graduated.

I shake the thought from my mind, unlock the door to my office, and consult my diary. It informs me that I have a new patient to see at 2 p.m.: Dominic Whiley, a man in his mid-twenties, originally from Manchester, but now residing at the halfway house in Lewannick Road, Swansburne. He suffers with auditory hallucinations, and has a file as thick as the Bible. He's been living with these symptoms for years, and he's been referred to me by Faye Farefield. I've known Faye for years – she's an excellent GP who doesn't prevaricate with following the process when she can see that intervention is required. There's no reason I shouldn't be able to help Dominic. He appears to have stopped taking his medication, for reasons which I will have to ascertain, but he has responded well to risperidone in the past, so I'll prescribe some more, as well as a week's worth of zopiclone, perhaps, so he can catch up on some sleep. I also hope to encourage him to join the 'hearing voices' group that's held in Totnes every Wednesday morning: schizophrenia, like most mental illnesses, actually, can be isolating.

The clock ticks its way round to 5 p.m. I am sitting at my desk, staring at the computer screen, trying to update my log. My desk is usually tidy, but today my books are strewn over it, with yellow Post-its marking relevant pages. I have a dancing flower on my desk, and I drum a beat out on the mahogany to watch it writhe. There are some in the department who consider it 'unprofessional', but I believe it humanises me, and it has to be more conducive to recovery than the cheaply framed watercolours of Victorian hunting scenes that someone has seen fit to hang everywhere.

I've followed this career path for twenty-two years now, and it still fascinates me. You give similar sets of symptoms the same name, but the way in which the illness manifests itself – the way it affects its host, if you will – is unique. Dominic arrived late, so I hadn't seen him in the waiting room. When I opened the heavy door and called his name, he stood shakily, clutching the mandatory 'how-are-you-now?' form in his fist. He presented as distressed. His head twitched in the same way a horse flicks its tail to brush off flies. His gaze darted around the room, but he held his free hand out to shake mine. He made brief eye contact and flashed me an even briefer smile. I offered him the armchair opposite mine. I faced the window; he faced my desk, and addressed the dancing flower or the floor rather than me. I glanced over his questionnaire and wondered to what extent he'd lied. He was nervous; distracted. At one point he began to rock in the chair, but he caught himself and grinned. He said that, yes, he heard voices, but he wouldn't do what they said. He frowned and twitched his head again. He said that he was okay, and that although the voices had bothered him in the past, he could "live with them now". He admitted that he wasn't sleeping very well. When I broached the subject of medication, Dominic replied that he didn't need it because he was "okay with everything", and that it had made him feel "slow and foggy" when he needed to be "sharp". I asked him what he meant by that, but he offered no explanation, and just shook his head. The jumper he was wearing didn't fit him properly and he kept pulling his sleeves down. I noticed several recent slashes on his forearms. I was honest with him and said that the voices were clearly upsetting him and that recommencing risperidone would help him as it had in the past, but that he could try olanzapine to see if that worked better for him. His face brightened a bit at that suggestion, so I wrote him a prescription for the drug, adding two zopiclone tablets to give him a couple of nights' good sleep. I really didn't want him to be in possession of any more than that.

Zopiclone – if only I could prescribe some for myself! I can't remember the last time I slept well. I lie awake for hours, trying to block out the sound of Julia's snoring – it doesn't matter what time I go to bed, whether I read or not, whether I drink coffee past 8 p.m. or not – and when I have managed to fall asleep, I wake to see that the red numbers on my alarm clock have only increased by one or two. I am an intelligent, almost-middle-aged man; I've had a long and expensive education; I am a psychiatrist – I am well aware that there are aspects of my life that I need to address. Yet I find myself taking longer than necessary to gather my things, lock my office and exit the hospital. When I get to my car, I notice a piece of paper stuck under my windscreen wipers, and curse myself for forgetting to pop down and buy a second parking ticket, but thankfully the traffic warden has taken pity on me and just left me a note which reads, 'you owe me a pint'. I smile at this, wishing I could just go to the pub, but I know Julia would smell alcohol on me and tut, so using the steering wheel as a table, I draft some notes in preparation for the lecture I have to give next month. Twilight has fallen when I pull out of the hospital car park, and I turn right instead of left, taking the long way home. A group of girls are standing outside that youth-club pub, The Riverboat – all legs and high heels. One of them waves at me as I approach the roundabout at the corner. I slow to a stop, and smile back, my hand on the button to lower the window; then I realise the girl is Candy, mouth a 'see you tomorrow' and drive off. She would say that it's 'dimpsy'. All I want to do is dump the car and join her for a drink. But I have to go home to Julia.

When Julia and I realised that our relationship was serious, I initiated what she called a 'deep and meaningful' conversation while we were enjoying a coffee after an al fresco lunch at a restaurant on Cathedral Green, in Exeter. I was trying to reiterate how important my career was to me, how I would be working long hours for the rest of our life together, and, arguably more importantly, that I had no desire to become a father. Julia was nodding, but I could see that she was off in a daydream about our impending engagement. I reached over and took her hand in an attempt to make her consider my view seriously – I even said the words 'as a woman'. She looked me in the eyes – she was so young and fresh and pretty – and she said that she understood, and that she felt the same way. "I love you, Erazmus," she said. "I'll never hold you back." I wanted her so badly, I chose to believe her.

Lizzie

My room at The Stables was, like all the rest, on the first floor. It had a sea green carpet, and contained a single bed, an old wooden wardrobe, a low, oval coffee table, a chair, a bedside table and a sink for brushing your teeth and washing your face in, or as in the case of my fellow inmate and friend, Sophie, extinguishing contraband joss sticks. It's one of the most homely institutions in which I've resided. When I arrived, I was glad to see, by the grey-blue remains stuck to the bare wall, that you were allowed to use Blu Tack. Wherever I am, and I've lived in a lot of places, I cover the walls with articles from newspapers, photos, and things I've written and drawn. I'm trying to find the meaning of it all, the core, and I look for clues and patterns. Today I'm adding to it – I'm drawing the view from my window. It's pretty, with a clear sky; the garden slopes steeply up to the greenhouse, ending in a hawthorn hedge that masks the fence and the wall. You'd have to be really determined to climb that fence – you'd get cut to shreds. The Stables is like our own little planet; a place of safety, protected from the madness of the universe beyond by brambles, wire mesh and stone. Something glints on the top of the wall, though – I think it's glass shards.

I'm sitting in my chair looking out of the permanently closed window, drawing the garden with its sparkly-topped wall, when I see him. Dom. I know it's him. Adrenaline rushes through me, and I have to catch my breath. He has his back to me, facing the wall, and he's with Dunstan, who must be showing him round, pointing out the greenhouse, like he did with me, like they do with everybody – we can grow our own tomatoes, or plants for the garden; it's therapeutic, wholesome. Normal. Dom's in his usual black T-shirt and jeans and his hair is the same – short at the back and floppy round the front – although the red is almost faded out. As he turns, I see that he has lost weight – he must be on different meds. I rush to the sink and splash water on my face, brush my teeth and make my eyes up. I use a lot of eyeliner, and I'm relieved I manage to get it on right in my hurry. Then I change my T-shirt, brush my hair, and go downstairs; my body tense, my forehead beginning to get hot. I hear Dunstan's rasping laugh, and track it to the front room. They both have a coffee now and are sitting on the sofa, smoking. I enter the room shakily, feeling in my jeans pocket for my baccy. I know that I'm blushing – I'm so self-conscious I could die, so I concentrate on rolling my cigarette. I sit in the armchair adjacent to Dom, and glance at him with something that I hope resembles welcoming gladness. I spark up my rollie, and there's a pause in their conversation. Dom registers me with a shy smile. He has a small mouth, like a rosebud. I move my focus to his eyes, and they pull me in as they dilate.

"Hi," I say, smiling properly now. "What happened to you?" It's not what I meant to say, but it comes out because the attraction is still there; I can feel it. Dunstan is speaking. Dom has been discharged from the AAU at Torquay, and he's coming to live here.

"I stopped taking my meds," Dom says, with a wry raise of his eyebrows, and we both have a little laugh at that. "I hated them – I still hate having to take them – you know what it's like – they make you slow and tired all the time, and I didn't have the energy to paint – I just sat there staring at TV all day, and that's not me – that's not living – it's pointless existence. I went cold turkey, and I was okay for a while – the voices were there, but I was all right, you know. And then it all got a bit fucked up, and me and Rebecca split up, and I was in hospital for a bit, and now I'm here – so I guess we'll be housemates again." Dom grins and stubs his cigarette out in the heavy, glass ashtray, giving it a twist, just to make sure.

Dunstan notices and cuts in brightly, "Glad to see you've got a friend here already, Dominic. Let's see if we can't get you back on track! Ready to go?"

And then they're gone.

It's my turn to do the front room, so I get the polish and the duster from the kitchen cupboard. First I empty all the ashtrays, resisting the urge to touch the butt Dom has just extinguished. I bet it's still warm. There's no one else in the room now, which makes things easier. I do the windowsills, then the fireplace, the coffee tables, underneath and the legs as well, then the telly, then the bookcase. I can't be bothered to take all the books off and dust each one – I'm never sure how thorough they expect you to be. Bonnie appears and engages me in conversation, trying to distract me from my thoughts – she knows that I hate doing my chores because I feel pressure – everything is a seemingly unending, impossible task – and I know she's trying to make the moment better, but it actually makes it worse, because I never have anything to say, and then I have the additional worry that I am boring her. There's an awkward silence while I rack my brains for something interesting to say – the inside of my head like a loft with dust sheets again. Eventually, she leaves to put the kettle on, and I'm so relieved I let out the breath I hadn't realised I'd been holding. I plump up the cushions and put them back in their right places on the sofa. I hate cushions – they give me the creeps, and they always smell of old people. It's like that old Pulp song where Jarvis sings about figurines. Finally, I hoover up. People are gross, filthy, smelly things that make gross, filthy, smelly messes; we spend our days making messes and cleaning them up, washing ourselves only to get sticky again after a sleep; the monotony and futility of it all makes me want to die. I feel like Esther in *The Bell Jar*; like Elizabeth in *Prozac Nation* – I want to wash once and be done with it forever.

Eventually, the front room is passable, and I'll earn my £2 for completing my chores this week. The money always goes to my cigarette fund. I took up smoking cigarettes in my twenties. I'd been smoking dope with my friends for years, but I got paranoid that it was reacting with my antidepressants, so I gave it up. The trouble was, I was hooked, so I started smoking straights, but quickly found this was too expensive, so I moved on to rollies. I love the process of getting out the paper, the sharp sound as it comes out of the packet, lining up a filter, then sprinkling a pinch of tobacco, just enough, not too much to make it too fat, or too little to make what Dom always called 'prison rollies'. I wonder how he knew. Last week, my folks came to visit, and Mum slipped me a couple of packets of Silk Cut while Dad wasn't looking. I used to prefer them, but they always feel really big in your mouth after rollies, so I smoked one and sold the rest to Lydia.

Mum and Dad visit once a week. They like to take me out, to the seaside usually, if it's nice, for chips or ice cream. I'm allowed to go out with them now – they are trusted to look after me, and I am trusted not to run off and kill myself while I'm out with them – but I'm not allowed out on my own. It's lucky I like drawing and reading. Was it Emerson who asked why go out, when you can go everywhere in your head, or something like that? The trouble is, I don't like what's in my head. I've moved around a lot, hoping a new town will magic me into a new person, but you take yourself with you – hence the drugs and alcohol. Obviously, I don't have any way of self-medicating here, so when the front of my head gets hot, all I can do is rub it, but I just end up making my forehead red, and then they tell me off. However, after seeing Dom again, and with my chore done, I don't feel too bad. Bonnie brings me a coffee, and I take it outside, under the fragrant wisteria, and smoke, staring at the orange fish in the black pond, letting the tension in my body dissipate. There is still no one around, which is weird because there's usually someone roaming about at all hours. I'm enjoying the birdsong and the sounds of the cars on the road below. Peaceful sounds. Bonnie plonks herself down in the wrought iron chair next to mine. I almost scream at her to leave me alone.

"So how do you feel, having Dom come to live here?" she asks. Ah. It's going to be one of those chats.

"I don't know. I mean, it's nice – hopefully we can be friends again."

"'Nice'? Wasn't he the reason you ended up in hospital that time?"

"Yes and no. I was ill. It wasn't his fault. He and Rebecca were together; I should have just accepted that. It wasn't her fault. Anyway, Dom said they split up."

There's a pause.

"Yeah. I know," Bonnie says. She wants to tell me something, I know she does. I don't know what to do, so I roll another cigarette.

"Look, Lizzie, I can't say much, because of the confidentiality thing, but Heather wasn't keen on him coming here – because of what happened with you two, and you were here first, obviously. But you know what it's like with the NHS – too many people need help, and there are only so many houses like this; there aren't enough CPNs, and it was deemed that Dom needed twenty-four-hour supervision, but there was someone else who needed his hospital bed more than he did – The Stables was the only option. If Dom's being here makes things difficult for you – in any way – let us know, and we'll work something else out. Okay?" She looks me full in the face, and I can see that's she's genuinely concerned. I smile.

"Thanks, Bonnie, but it will be okay. Don't worry."

It's my cook day today. I wake up with that sick lurching in my stomach, and I want to run away. I push the feeling down and drink my coffee by the pond as usual, but I can't stop the tears. Someone touches my shoulder – it makes me jump. It's Bonnie.

"I'll help you," she says, straight off the bat. "We'll do beans on toast for lunch; and quiche, salad and chips for dinner." I turn and smile at her through the tears. Why is this such a big deal for me? I'm so ashamed – a pathetic excuse for a human being, using up someone else's air – using up someone's place here at The Stables. I should just do everyone a favour and kill myself.

Reluctantly, I go downstairs after my shower and into the dreaded kitchen. I get the plates and two large saucepans out, and put two tins of beans in each. I mean I stand the tins in the pans. I don't know why I do it, but it feels like the right thing to do. Inevitably, Dunstan comes in to make me feel like shit.

"Ah, good, good," he says, grinning. "Cordon-bleu lunch again today! I think you're supposed to remove the beans from the tins, though, Lizzie. Maybe I should ask Lydia to give you a hand!" Lydia has just poured some fresh coffee from a cafetiere; she keeps her eyes on the floor and walks quickly out of the kitchen.

I don't like Dunstan – he gives me the creeps for one thing; he reminds me of Jabba the Hutt. And I don't think Heather would like it if she heard him talking to the patients like that – he's like it with all of us - but he's always nice when she's around. I think he makes Lydia uncomfortable, too – I'm sure he touched her bum on purpose when he brushed past her just now. I ought to say something, but what if I'm wrong? Poor Lydia – she's not doing so well at the moment – her 'shadows' are back. I follow her into the front room, and she sits next to Heather, who's reading some papers on the sofa. Not knowing what else to do, I offer Lydia a rollie, knowing she only smokes straights. She smiles, shakes her head, and her eyes well up, and she starts rocking back and forth. Heather looks concerned, and puts a hand on Lydia's shoulder. Lydia lets out a sob, and lights one of her own cigarettes with shaking hands. The urge to tell Heather about Dunstan rises in me, but what if I'm imagining it, and what if it makes Lydia more upset? I don't want to get anyone in trouble. I also don't want them to think I'm getting worse.

I'm functioning, but I'm not getting any better. I feel like a fraud, because everyone seems to have worse problems than me. I go to my evening sessions with Phee, and I go to my CSA group in Totnes, but I find myself acting a bit – I don't want the group leader, or Phee, to feel like they're not succeeding in their jobs – I'm smiling, and saying that I think I can forgive my grandfather now; that I understand why I am the way I am; that life is beautiful, really, and I'm going to get better, find a job, live independently, blah, blah, blah; when in fact I spent the whole train journey down here planning where and when to slit my wrists. There never seems to be a good time.

I met with my psychiatrist, Dr Whittle, again, and he wants me to continue on my cocktail of meds. I like him, and if I'm honest, I feel more comfortable talking to him than to Phee; if I'm really honest, sometimes when we're talking, I get a warm flush and have to try to keep myself from blushing. I have to look at the floor. I should probably ask to see another psychiatrist, because getting thoughts like these can't be good for my recovery, but then I always get 'intrusive thoughts', and I do enjoy our sessions in a weird way. In fact, I look forward to them. Dr Whittle genuinely wants me to 'recover' – he never says 'get better' or anything like that. He comes out to The Stables almost daily, to see how we're all doing, and to talk with Heather and the team – it's like a ward round. It also means that he can see us for our sessions at The Stables, and that no one has to drive us out to his office in Eskwich – I had to go there once for a med review when I was in the AAU, because I was a 'priority' and he had too many patients booked in to drive down. I wonder how many offices he has – does he have one in every hospital? I hear myself ask, "Do you have a dancing flower in all your offices?"

Dr Whittle laughs. "No, just the one in Eskwich. It can get a bit bleak there, and I need something to cheer me up!"

"Tell me about it. I was born and raised there!"

"Yes, I know," he says, tapping his notebook with his expensive pen, smiling. Of course he does. There's a pause. "Lizzie? How are you getting on with Phee?"

"Okay, I suppose," I say to the beige carpet. Dr Whittle waits for me to elaborate. "It's just I've told so many people about my life, and it's never really helped, and I get bored of talking about it. I kind of shut off a bit, and Phee thinks maybe I'm on too many meds to connect properly with the work we're doing ... I'm just kind of going along with it, really."

"Do you think you might find it easier to talk to me?" Dr Whittle asks.

"Umm ..."

"Not about the abuse and the way your illness has manifested, specifically – more what it was like for you growing up, what your family dynamic was like ..." And then he says in a ridiculous accent, "Tell me about your mother." It's so unexpected and funny that we both start laughing. His eyes flash for a second, and I wonder if he likes me. I shake my head to clear it – of course he doesn't. He's probably like this with all his patients; and in any case, I'm too young.

Dom has moved in, and it's been nice, sitting by the pond with him, or walking round the garden, or even just watching some crappy film in the front room together in the evenings. We've got the same twisted sense of humour. Sometimes, if I catch him rocking and shaking his head, I'll sit next to him, and start making a soap opera of what's going on in the fish tank, doing different voices for each of the fish. The angel fish is a narcissist, the neons are a gang of chavs, and the slug-type thing that eats the algae off the sides of the tank, I call Droopy, because he reminds me of the cartoon bloodhound, and he is clinically depressed. It makes Dom laugh, anyway, and I'm glad about that, but what I'm really thinking is that I wish it was me and Dr Whittle sitting here. I've started calling him Erazmus, in my head.

Don't get me wrong. I still think Dom's gorgeous, and I'd rather be in his company than anyone else's, but he doesn't give much back. He chats more than he used to, but he tends to repeat himself, and it often brings me down. He must have told me about when Rebecca tried to kill herself a million times. Maybe it's affected him more deeply than I thought. But then I never liked Rebecca. What happened was, Dom's voices took him over when he stopped taking his meds, and they kept telling him that Rebecca was seeing someone else. Dom found this plausible, because Rebecca was recovering well; she'd started a college course, and had got a voluntary job in the Oxfam shop down the road. Dom got all Mr Hyde about it, Rebecca started drinking again, and then one day she booked a room in a B & B, in Bishopsham of all places, got the train there, with her rucksack full of vodka, rope and razor blades, got pissed, cut herself to ribbons, and finally tried to hang herself. The only reason she didn't pull it off was because she didn't think to draw the curtains. Some perv who lived in the top-floor flat of the building opposite the B & B had been watching her through his binoculars, getting himself off, but when Rebecca stood on a chair and tried to attach the rope to the hefty Victorian light fitting, he called the police and ran over the road to get the owners to break into her room. Consequentially, she got an emergency section and was taken to Exeter, and Dom ended up voluntary in Torquay.

Suicide – it's all in the details. I wonder what happened to the perv.

Dr Whittle comes and finds me, wherever I am in The Stables, whenever he visits – regardless if we have a scheduled session or not – just to see how I'm doing – and I put my make-up on every day, just in case. He's like a rainbow to me, and I look for him when the darkness descends. To be honest, it rarely lifts. I just want this shit in my head gone. But I see the patterns; I recognise the symbolism. It makes me smile. This is how things are supposed to be, and I am comforted. Even though I've showered and changed my clothes, I can still smell the smoke. Even though he's my psychiatrist, I know Dr Whittle and I are in love.

I started a fire. It was supposed to be a small, controlled one, lasting just as long as it took me to burn a photo, a book, and a necklace – a symbolic gesture that I hoped was going to cure me. I got the idea from my child sexual abuse therapy group; we'd smashed a load of plates in a 'safe and

30

controlled environment' but that hadn't done a thing for me – probably because it had been safe and controlled – so I spoke to the group leader, who suggested a safe and controlled fire. The symbolism appealed to me – burning my hell – so I made my plans, and selected the three things that I wanted to throw into the flames. The photo was one taken when I was a child, at Christmas time, with my parents and grandparents in 1970s jumpers; the book was a fat Sherlock Holmes anthology that my grandfather had been obsessed with; he had suggested I read it, and virtually forced the thing into my hands; the necklace was the gold and opal one he'd bought for my grandmother on one of their wedding anniversaries. I didn't want to part with it – after all, Grandma had passed it to on me, and she had been the most wonderful person I had ever met, and I missed her so much it actually hurt my chest sometimes – but the necklace had been contaminated by her husband, my grandfather, as I had. War hero or not, he should have been the one who got locked up, not me, but he died before I started getting the flashbacks. He must have carried that opal around wrapped in a bay leaf all my childhood – how else had he managed to stay invisible?

In all honesty, I didn't really want to destroy anything, because then it would be gone and I'd have nothing tangible to remind me that it had all been real, but I was simultaneously desperate to be free from the torture that was going on in my head. I didn't ever expect a fire started with some twigs, last week's copy of the Gazette and a box of Swan Vestas to get hot enough to melt gold, or even to consume the hardback cover of the book – it was more of a cleansing-by-fire ritual, and I'd intended to throw the remains off the end of Tamehaven Pier and into the sea with the ashes. I had a litre bottle of Evian with me to extinguish the flames when I was finished; to my mind, measures were in place so that the ritual would be safe and controlled.

Fate, however, had other ideas. June, July and August had been unusually dry – here, down in dear old Devon, where it rains six days out of seven – and now we were enjoying an Indian summer. I made the fire on a patch of weedy grass up in the garden, but the grass was yellow and crispy, and something in the fire popped; a spark flew off and landed on the desiccated remains of a raspberry bush, and by the time I realised what was happening, my bottle of water was rendered obsolete. In panic, I looked around wildly for a watering can, a hose, something, anything, and I screamed down to the house on instinct, though I knew no one would hear me. Tears soon glued my hair to my cheeks as I looked helplessly on, frozen; but suddenly Dr Whittle was there, hauling me back down the slope to the safety of the house and depositing me there, heaving up the fire extinguisher that was somehow on the path. I watched, stunned, as he ran part of the way back up and blasted water on the flames.

It was a sunny Saturday in late October. I'd chosen that day because there was only a skeleton staff on duty. Most of them had gone off on a day trip with the other residents, which meant I was unlikely to be disturbed; also, I wouldn't give anyone vulnerable any dangerous ideas. When a dishevelled Dr Whittle and I came inside, Bonnie accosted us and demanded to know what the hell had just happened – the smell of the smoke had reached her and she said she was sure as hell I hadn't burnt any toast – and Dr Whittle, in his calming, professional manner, told her that he'd been supervising me; that I'd mentioned the idea of burning a couple of things in a symbolic cleansing ritual, during our scheduled review; that he'd concluded that as the other residents were away, today was, in all likelihood, the only day I'd be able to carry out the ritual; that because we'd been working together for many months, it made sense for him to supervise me; and that he'd had the fire extinguisher on hand, in case of such an eventuality. Bonnie had stood there, clearly in a quandary, but Dr Whittle massively outranked her, so she couldn't do anything but inform Heather, when she returned to work the Monday after, and was forced to admit that she'd been having a sneaky coffee in the kitchen at the time, while things were quiet, as she had just done six night shifts in a row and she was knackered. Heather wasn't happy, but couldn't do anything about it – after all, she had a duty of care to her staff, as well as the patients.

I'd overheard some of their conversation, and walked quickly away to get on with my designated chore, but Heather pulled me into the dining room to 'have a quick word', just as I was about to sit in the lounge with a coffee and a cigarette. I was scared there'd be repercussions; however, Dr Whittle was a respected consultant psychiatrist who Heather had worked with for many years, and despite the fact that what he'd done had been way out of his remit, Heather said she had no choice but to let it go – after all, there was no way she'd be allowed to recruit more support staff – and I didn't have my freedom restricted.

Dr Whittle and I now shared a secret; and although it was unspoken, I saw it reflected in his eyes that something had changed for both of us by the greenhouse and the dead raspberry bushes, under that crystal autumn sky.

The Indian summer is finally over, and proper Octobery weather has set in; every day is blustery and wet. Fiery-coloured leaves shine with rain, and flap about on the paths like injured birds. I'm 'struggling' today, as Bonnie puts it, and when Dunstan and Dom come back from doing the shopping chore, Dom presents me with a box of Maltesers. I'm curled up on the sofa reading *Dracula* again, doodling pictures of how I see his face in my mind's eye, when Dr Whittle breezes in and perches himself on the edge of the adjacent armchair. I feel his presence before I see him, and enjoy the warmth of the smile he brings to my face. And then suddenly Dom is here, all smiles, giving me what is essentially a romantic box of chocolates. It surprises me, and I automatically smile at the gesture, but I don't want them!

Time slows down, but this does nothing to help me. Dom is grinning, but I still haven't taken the proffered red box from his hands, because I can feel Dr Whittle's eyes boring into my skull, but what can I do? I thank Dom for being thoughtful and trying to cheer me up, but Dr Whittle's eyes are on mine, and I try to send him a psychic message that there's nothing going on between me and Dom, but Dom sits down beside me and starts telling me about how he hadn't freaked out in the supermarket, and I'm trying to smile at him, but send my message to Dr Whittle at the same time, but Dr Whittle sighs and shakes his head and says, "I'll catch up with you next time, Lizzie. Enjoy your chocolates," and walks out.

And when I storm up to my room after my seven o'clock session with Phee, I smash my water glass in my sink, select a shard, and cut myself.

Erazmus

I pride myself on being in control of my emotions and my actions. I couldn't have become consultant psychiatrist if I wasn't – I wouldn't be able to help my patients; I wouldn't be able to cope with what I deal with every day of my working life; and I would be a hypocrite, and thus unfit for the position.

Having said that, I am human.

Julia wants children. I knew this would happen. I went over and over this, telling her that I wasn't ever going to want any, that I wanted to concentrate on my career and do my bit for humanity that way – I went over and over it, to make sure she understood and was happy, before I asked her to marry me. I loved her – I wanted her to be fulfilled. I wanted us to be on the same page. Seven years into our marriage, we adopted a kitten from a rescue centre. 'Fly' was lithe, playful, companionable; his short black coat shone and his yellow eyes blazed. He liked sitting on our laps in the evening. I thought that was our family; I thought that was enough. Julia didn't. Julia thought that was the start.

Yesterday, in my scheduled session with Lizzie, at The Stables, I found myself asking her if she'd like to come to the beach with me on my day off.

Lizzie

I don't think this is legal – I know he'd get struck off if anyone found out. It's a bright, cold, Friday in January, and I have been doing so well, I have been allowed out on my own for a few hours. I have to be back at lunch time. I tell Heather that I am taking the train to Tamehaven, and in doing so, realise that I never disposed of the remains of the items I burnt in the fire. I'd stuffed them into a shopping bag, hidden them in the bottom of my wardrobe and forgotten all about them. Deciding to take them with me, I scrabble about until I find the bag. It stinks of smoke; I wonder if my room smells, and I've just grown used to it. I wish I could open my bedroom window, and make a mental note to buy some air freshener. Leaving the grounds of The Stables alone for the first time in months, I walk quickly down the hill, through town, and out to the park, opposite the railway station. Dr Whittle – Erazmus – is waiting in the car park, leaning against his car, scanning the scene. He spots me, smiles widely, and waves me over. My legs feel like jelly, and my cheeks are hot. Erazmus walks around to my side of the car and opens the door for me. No one's ever done that before, and I stumble into the car, getting my legs caught up with the strap of my handbag. He drives a black Mercedes, a smart yet anonymous car, and when he gets in, he asks me what music I'd like to listen to. I am shy and awkward, so I say I don't know, and he laughs and puts the radio on. It's Oasis – *Cigarettes and Alcohol*. He nods at the rollie I'm twirling in my hands, and then to the four-pack of cider sitting on the back seat. I laugh, stash the cigarette in my bag and begin to relax. He asks me what's in the bag, so I tell him, and he suggests we go to the pier and finish the ritual, which returns

36

us to our roles as psychiatrist and patient; he asks the questions, I give hesitant answers, until I blurt out an apology for spoiling his day off by making him work. This amuses him, and he assures me that today is not work, that he never thinks of it as work when he's with me, and he reaches his hand over and takes mine. A small gesture, but it's electric. Then he takes his hand away with a quick, nervous smile.

The journey to Tamehaven doesn't take long. Erazmus parks up the far end of the big car park that overlooks the sea and the Ness. He takes a rucksack out of the boot, buys a parking ticket, and leads me down to the back beach where people's small boats seem to climb up the sandbank like turtles. There's driftwood, shells, seaweed, and gulls and terns swoop and shriek. There's also sea glass, which reminds me of Dom, and I can't stop myself picking a bit up and putting it in my pocket to give to him later. Erazmus smiles – he must think that I'm picking it up as a souvenir of our day together, and now I want to throw it away, but I can't. I feel the familiar sting of tears.

Erazmus notices the change in my mood, and suggests we have a hot drink, so we go into a jewel of a pub, called The Ship, which backs onto the beach. We have coffee first, and later a cider, and we share a bowl of chips. And soon we're swapping histories, and we're sitting so close we're almost touching. I know I shouldn't be drinking on my meds, and I know he shouldn't be drinking because he's driving, but a reckless spirit has taken over us, and we don't care.

It's warm in the sunshine and we feel better, so we go back outside, lay our blanket down on the sand, and sit with our backs against the warmed-up wall. Erazmus delves into his rucksack again and snaps two of the cans of cider out of the plastic ring holding the four-pack together and hands one to me. He cracks his open, swigs from it, and says, "Let's go for a paddle," and he grabs my free hand, pulls us both to standing, laughing, and we stumble down towards the water, the soft sand becoming wet sand, and then we're splashing in the gentle surf of the back beach. He reaches into the shallow water, takes out an almost heart-shaped piece of sea glass, and hands it to me, smiling triumphantly like a little boy who's ridden his bike without stabilisers for the first time. Ironically, this destroys the moment, as it makes me think of Dom and The Stables and my bag of charred remains abandoned with our shoes next to the blanket; we realise that the morning is getting old and we need to bury my past, which is also our beginning, at sea.

We pack up and hurry back to the seafront, and onto the pier. I pretend to myself that this is not just rushed, that it's still romantic, and try to convince Erazmus, with a hopeful smile.

There are groups of people at the very end of the pier, and we have to wait until they've gone before we can complete what has become 'our' ritual. We can both feel the seconds slipping by, knowing we have to get back to the car fast if I am to be back at The Stables on time. If I'm not on time, I run the risk of not being allowed out alone again. The three boys who've clearly bunked off school, finish scratching their names into the damp, salt-laden wooden boards, and slope off; we hear them giving each other dead arms until they disappear into the arcade. A baby's cry forces the pram-pushing mums to extinguish their cigarettes and leave. The old lady with the little dog shivers and heads inside.

Eventually the smart man in the dress-coat, who's been leaning over the railings, staring into the waves, straightens up and strides off, his highly polished shoes glinting in the sunshine. Erazmus suddenly stiffens and takes a step away from me, and the man gives him a curt nod as he passes. I'm about to ask if he knows that man, but when I look up at him, he is smiling again, and we quickly take his place at the very end of the pier. Erazmus gasps when I simply empty the contents of the shopping bag into the sea. I don't notice where the necklace sinks, the dust of the photo and pages disintegrate on contact, and in seconds the blackened remains of the book's cover are consumed by the ocean.

"What are those yellow things floating on the water?" I ask Erazmus.

"I don't know," he says. "That bloke must have dropped

his chips. Come on, I'll buy us an ice cream."

But there's not enough time for him to drop me at the station and for me to walk back up to The Stables as we'd planned, so Erazmus drives me as far up the hill as he dares, and parks on a side street. We sit in the car for a moment, silent, thinking about what we've just done, and then he leans over, cups my face with his hand, and kisses me.

I take my place at the dining table at The Stables, and Heather nods at me approvingly. I force down cheese salad sandwiches with the rest of them. Dom asks how my first morning of freedom was, and I give him the piece of sea glass; which is absolutely the worst thing I could have done.

It's seven o'clock and Phee comes into the front room to call me for our session. A few weeks have passed since my morning in Tamehaven, and although I'm ecstatic because Erazmus and I are in love, I'm worrying about Dom – he's getting sketchier by the day. Whenever I turn around, he's there; whenever I look up from my book, he's staring at me; he keeps getting the sea glass I gave him out of his pocket and rubbing it over his rosebud mouth. I've asked Phee if she thinks Dom's okay, and said that I'm a bit worried, but she says he's not her patient, so she doesn't know, but even if she did, it would be against their code of ethics to disclose anything to me. She suggests I talk to Heather.

Our sessions, now we're in the depths of it, have become horrible. No one's ever dissected my past like this, so brutally, examining all my relationships so harshly – was I, amongst other things, jealous of my brother, my cousins, my friends? Was that a contributing factor? Was I groomed? What the hell kind of a question was that? I could tell by the look in Phee's eyes that she knew she was pushing me, pushing me to places in my brain I had never been. I also knew she was doing it because she genuinely wanted me to exorcise my demons. But no one had asked me questions like this. I love my family. Through it all, I've always had them, and even when we've fallen out and stuff, they've always done their best for me; we've always picked up the pieces. How can I say anything other than good things about the only stable thing in my life? It feels like a betrayal. I come out of our sessions blotchy faced and shaking. It's all so raw.

And when I see Erazmus at The Stables, I just want him to put his arms around me and make it go away for a moment, but he is the consummate professional there; he says the work I'm doing with Phee is essential to my recovery, and if I don't do it now, how many more years am I going to spend in and out of hospitals, waiting for memories to come back when they might never return because they might destroy me if they did; there's only recovery, never a cure, is his mantra. Didn't I know that I couldn't have it both ways? He made me cry when he said that. How can he be so harsh? To me? I know he's struggling with the conflict between our private and professional relationships, but sometimes it hurts me so much that I think that he is on their side, that he will always be on their side, that he can talk to all the psychos he likes, but he will never understand what it is to live with the horrors in our heads. Big, thick books will give you case studies, observations made by men who have their own agendas. They're a different breed: us and them.

Then again, I can't demonise them – I'm a 'voluntary' patient here, not like poor Lydia, kept at The Stables by law, not free will, while her life crumbles around her. I was sat out by the pond with her one evening, just smoking in companionable silence, under the scent of the wisteria, when she said, "He's left me." She meant her fiancé. I just put my hand on her shoulder as she took a long drag on her cigarette. I didn't say anything – there was nothing to say. After a while, she stood up shakily and went indoors, back up to her room. I just sat there.

I'm sitting on the wrought iron chair, thinking about this, thinking about everything, for some minutes, and then I hear the front door open and close quietly. I turn around in my chair, flicking some ash, and am glad to see it's Dom. I give him a warm smile. He scrapes the other chair over, closer to mine so he's sitting right next to me, and holds my hand on

40

my lap. He says, "You look like you could use a drink," and I give him a wobbly smile, being on the verge of tears again. He says he's smuggled a bottle of vodka into his room. I look at him.

"Really?" He says yes. He says I should come and have some, and relax and forget it all for a while. He's got some lemonade to mix it with. And against my better judgement, in fuck-it mode, and because it's Them and Us, and it will never be any different, I follow him inside and up the stairs.

It's still light, but it must be getting on for about nine o'clock now. Everyone's in the front room watching *Toy Story* again, and no one sees us as we go up to his room. It's on the opposite side of the house to mine, and looks out over the front garden and the road that curves steeply uphill. In contrast to mine, his room is an absolute tip – clothes and shoes everywhere – but the pictures and articles cut out and stuck up around his bed are similar. We're both looking for the answers.

Dom really is a very talented artist – there are sketches of people and plants, and, disconcertingly, there's one of me in profile. I don't mention it, though, because he's handed me a red plastic mug full of vodka and lemonade. I ask him how he got it into the house, and he says his sister brought it in, disguised as a bottle of Evian. All gifts are checked before they're given to us (I wasn't allowed the framed photograph of Stonehenge in moody lighting because the glass at the front was chipped, and this might be too tempting a sharp surface for someone desperate) and I don't quite trust that this is the truth, but I am angry with Erazmus, and with the system, and I feel the blackness sweeping over me again. I look about for a place to sit down, and Dom shoves am armful of T-shirts off the bed and onto the floor, and sits down, patting the space next to him. And this is how I come to be drunk at The Stables.

No matter how much he's been freaking me out recently, as I relax we find we have a lot to talk about together, and as it grows dimpsy he puts some music on low – trance stuff that I don't recognise – and draws the flimsy green curtains.

41

We're drinking quickly and soon we're laughing, trying to stifle the sound, and then I'm crying again and his hand is on my bare shoulder, playing with the straps of my bra and vest top. And this is how we come to have sex, on the unmade bed amidst the sketches and the piles of dark clothes; just once, just quickly, before we have time to think about what we're doing. And then I come to, and panic because it must be late and I haven't taken my meds.

Dom is asleep, naked, on top of the bed; I'm somehow still in my vest top, and I grab my bra and pull my jeans on, stuffing my socks into a pocket, open the door gingerly and then go to my room where I strip-wash, and brush my teeth. Then I go downstairs, for a glass of water, bumping into Dunstan, saying I fell asleep, but it's not too late to be thought odd, so he goes off to the office to get my meds – one long white capsule, two half-red-half-blues, a half-red-half-yellow, one little pink one, and two white ones, one circular, one long – lithium that stick to your tongue and are hard to swallow. All these are dropped into a little clear plastic thimble.

In hospital, when it's time for meds, they make you sit on a stool in the middle of a usually locked room, under harsh lights, and they watch you take your pills, one at a time, so you can't stash them under your tongue or hide them in your fist; and there are three members of staff present: one to watch, one to dispense, and one to fill in the paperwork. Here, it's more relaxed – you're supposedly more stable and can be trusted. But when Dunstan's on duty, he gives you your pills any time after nine o'clock when he happens to see you, so I have time to take mine, then go back upstairs and knock on Dom's door, shake him by the shoulder to wake him up, get himself dressed, spray himself with Lynx Africa and go down to take his meds. He groggily does so, and Dunstan is so engrossed in some TV programme that's on, sitting next to an uncomfortable-looking Lydia, that he doesn't notice that anything's amiss. In fact, once he's dispensed Dom's olanzapine and a sleeping tablet, he virtually sits on Lydia's lap, brushing her thigh with his hand as he relaxes. At this, Lydia shoots up, saying she's going to get a cup of coffee. She looks worried, harassed. I give her a searching glance and say that I'll join her, but before we go to the kitchen, we both gravitate to the front door, out by the pond. We spark up and stare at the slow, orange fish.

Erazmus

I'm worried about Lizzie, and how she's coping with her sessions with Phee. It is very difficult to be her psychiatrist at the same time as being her – what? – lover? Almost. I have to calm myself and keep it all separate. I've met with Phee and Heather several times, and the fact that Lizzie has taken a turn for the worse isn't surprising, given what she's dealing with, and it is surely a sign that she is processing it emotionally. This is something she has to get through, and she will, and I will be there for her in the best way I can.

As regards Dominic Whiley, I've had a few meetings with him and he seems to be responding well to his medication, now we can be sure that he's getting it every day. He says he hasn't heard any voices now for over a week. This is encouraging, although I've suggested that he continues to attend the hearing voices group in Totnes. However, today he seems a little smug. He looked me in the eye, which would ordinarily be a good sign, but it was almost as if he was challenging me, like we're a pair of tomcats. I've asked Heather and her team to keep a close eye on him.

And as for my life, Julia is now demanding we try for a baby. I thought that she'd been pushy from the off, mentioning it at every opportunity; getting me to hold babies at christenings; cooing at the little shoes in shoe shops; talking endlessly about the children of friends of ours, how they, our friends, are running away from us, continuing their lines; how my mother would love to live to see grandchildren. In a classic reaction, the more she pushes, the more I back away. I've been collating my notes and case studies for an academic book I intend to publish. This was always how I was going to give something back. I will not be able to become a professor if all my days and nights are taken up raising a child and consoling an emotional wife. I've watched it happen to my colleagues, and the exceptional students I met at university. Watch one news bulletin, and you've got ten reasons why we should be carrying out random culling trials on our own species and not the badgers. Surely any sensible person can see that it's better to help those who are already here, rather than bring another person in to – potentially – suffer? Take Lizzie – born into a respectable family in a privileged part of the world, and still, there's someone there to destroy her life. I'm a doctor – I just want to make things better.

We have these conversations, Julia and I, usually after dinner when we're sitting at the table finishing our wine. She lost her temper with me yesterday evening, smashing her glass on the table and screaming, "How could you be so selfish?!" before flouncing off to the bedroom. Humans have achieved incredible things in terms of scientific advancement and art; it beggars belief why an ordinarily intelligent woman can't think logically about the state of our planet, and control her animal urges. She is the one being selfish, being hypocritical. I spent that night in the spare room.

I spend the nights that follow in the spare room, too, and my working days lengthen, as does the bitter silence in our marital home. I control my animal urges with thoughts of Lizzie, or Candy, or both; but mainly with Lizzie. I know Lizzie, and I care about her.

One Friday night at The Stables, Lizzie is in floods of tears before she even enters the room for our session. She is inconsolable, so I break protocol and go over to her on my knees and pull her head into my shoulder, where she sobs as if her heart was breaking, soaking my jumper and shirt. It is so painful for me to see her like this, that I begin to cry too. She notices, and that's when she tells me about Dominic, about the vodka – that's when she tells me she's pregnant.

Lizzie

It's all my fault. No matter what I do, it all goes wrong and it's always my fault. When he first prescribed me lithium, Erazmus advised me that it was best to stop taking my contraceptive pill. My GP, Dr Farefield, agreed, saying that as I wasn't having sex anyway (flashbacks of abuse had left me dead inside), I needn't worry about becoming pregnant. So I'd chucked the little lilac-coloured pills I'd been taking for I-don't-know-how-long in the bin. The thing was, from the moment I'd started on the pill, I'd stopped bothering with condoms. I know it was stupid; I could have caught anything. And that night with Dom, I'd been drunk and upset, and had just forgotten that I wasn't on the pill any more. I hadn't even thought about it the morning after.

When I was in the shower this morning, my body felt all tight and hot, and it was almost painful to wash my boobs. I thought I must be due on, so I checked my Tampax and towel supply, realised I still had loads of everything, and then it hit me that I hadn't had a period in ages. And it was like I'd been smacked in the face – I knew I was pregnant. I just knew it. Fucking stupid, stupid, stupid bitch!

I sat on the floor, sobbing, until I was aware that my arms were stinging, there was blood under my nails. With the realisation of what I'd done to myself, I could breathe and think clearly again. Pain has always brought me clarity. I knew I was going to have to tell Erazmus, and I decided to do it in our session this evening.

"Come on, Lizzie. I know there's something bothering you – it would be obvious to a complete stranger! What's wrong?"

Erazmus tries to take my hands which are clenched, sweating fists on my lap; on autopilot I tense up even more, and my fingernails stab my palms so hard that I gasp.

"Lizzie! For goodness' sake, what's the matter?!"

For a split second after I tell him, his face is distorted by confusion, anger, incredulousness, devastation. It makes me want to die. Then he shakes his head as if to clear it, and when his eyes meet mine and he smiles, Erazmus has gone and he is Dr Whittle again.

"The first thing you have to do," he says, "is be sure. You need to do a pregnancy test. Hopefully the change in your menstrual cycle is a consequence of the intense therapy you're engaged in; it could even be down to your medication. If the test is positive, then you'll have to decide what you want to do."

While I'm processing what he means by this, he continues. "You can't tell Dominic. Ever."

"What?!" Now I am incredulous. "Dom has a right to know – it's his baby as much as mine!"

And now, Dr Whittle is confused, and it dawns on me what he meant when he said I needed to decide what I want to do. It makes my blood run cold.

"As far as I am concerned, being pregnant means having a baby!" I almost shout at him, trying to suppress a shiver. We stare at each other in silence, wondering who we're actually staring at.

"Lizzie – you've hurt me more than you can ever know." The pain blazes in his eyes, and his face momentarily distorts again, before he stands and turns away from me. There's a pause. "Regretfully, I have to terminate this evening's session." He doesn't turn around, so I exit the room, almost doubled over with anger and shame.

Still reeling from my session with Erazmus yesterday, I dither for ages in front of the pregnancy test stand in Boots. It amuses me that right next to the long, thin blue boxes there are colourful rows of condoms. I have never felt more awkward. I'm sure someone I know will see me, someone like Bonnie who'll make a song and dance about it. But no one does. I pray that Erazmus is right, and my elusive period is due to the stress of the therapy, but in my heart of hearts, I know it isn't. I'm going to have Dom's baby, and he'll have to be told soon, before it becomes obvious. And then my fears flood in – will the baby be okay mentally? Can you pass on psychosis? If so, is it fair to bring that child into the world? My brain starts doing somersaults. I'd heard once that a mother with OCD, who had to check everything, saw her five-year-old in the kitchen just before they went out, opening and closing all the cupboards and calling out 'Checked!' as she went. And it's finally dawning on me in my sessions with Phee, that there is no magic potion that's going to cure me – I'm on all the pills, I've tried everything going over the years, in different combinations; and no one's going to take the monster out of my head – not Erazmus, not any mental healthcare professional – I just have to learn to manage it. I think that's what's meant by Acceptance and Commitment Therapy. And to get to this realisation it's taken how long? Almost a decade. And the thought of passing this on to a child – that's almost too much to bear. But while I hold the packet in my hand, there's still a chance that I'm not pregnant. A Schrodinger's Cat scenario. To prolong this hope, after buying the test, I catch the train to Swansburne.

Pregnancy tests are supposed to be easy. You don't need to go to the doctor's any more and get a blood test – all you have to do is pee on a stick. I actually laugh at the dichotomy of the gross, mundane act that seals your fate. I can't face the public loos – it doesn't seem right – so I turn and walk into the park, then across the grass to where the stream passes the ornamental duck enclosure, and watch the penned-in birds. The black swans have big cygnets with them and I enjoy watching the graceful family glide slowly on by. Then it occurs to me that they're not gliding – beneath the surface of the muddy water, their huge grey feet are paddling unceasingly. I laugh at the metaphor that fits my life so perfectly. I have to do this test as soon as possible, but I need a drink first. Which I guess is what landed me in this predicament in the first place.

It's landed me in all my predicaments. In the course of therapy, I'm beginning to see that I've spent my life avoiding bad feelings. It's an automatic response in me – don't like it, shut it down. I know that I use alcohol to escape the fear I feel, and that this reflex isn't working in my favour any more; if it ever had. But today I feel that the circumstances are exceptional, and that the baby can handle one cider. So I walk up to the pub that was round the corner from the halfway house on Lewannick Road, where I'd met and fallen in love with Dom. It's fitting, symbolic.

Stepping into the porch area, I swing open the arched doors to the bar, and wonder for the umpteenth time what had possessed the landlord to paint them that dirty shade of brown. It makes me feel a bit sick. It's almost the same colour as the muddy water of the stream. There's a new barmaid who doesn't recognise me, for which I'm thankful, so I order a pint and drink it in silence, thinking about Dom.

In Dom's eyes we've crossed a boundary now we've had sex, which makes us all but 'together'. He continues to sit next to me at mealtimes, and to try to help me with my chores, and I can't go out for a cigarette without him appearing behind me, offering me his lighter. I don't find this as irritating as I had before – I'm fond of him, and he does make me laugh. And I can't deny that he's gorgeous, and that, arguably, I have more in common with him than I do with Erazmus. But I love Erazmus – I want to be in a relationship with him, not Dom, and I certainly don't want to be the mother of Dom's child. Any child. But a life is growing inside me – I don't need the pregnancy test – I know – my boobs feel hot and sore – my whole body feels different. Would Erazmus bring up another man's child? Would we ever be together anyway? He'll lose his job – probably be struck off – and I know that his work's important to him. But is it more important to him than I am? I stare into my drink, realising that my glass is half empty. I down the rest of the amber liquid and make my way upstairs to the toilets. 'Amber'. Nice name for a girl.

This is it – the moment of truth. I bang the toilet door closed, and wince at the word someone's scrawled on the back of it – 'TWAT'. I ease my jeans down – is my bum bigger already? Once I've seen the result, I'll have to deal with the outcome. Some of my pee gets onto the stick, and after five seconds, I put it on top of the loo roll dispenser, on some loo roll, obviously. I take a sneaky glance at the tester before the time's up, but I needn't wait any longer – there's a cross in its window. I'm pregnant. I clutch the stick and stare at the window, counting out the last few seconds, willing one of the lines to disappear. It doesn't. I read the word on the door again, and let the tears fall.

I've never believed that abortion is wrong. I'm not a pro-lifer – but at the same time I know I'll never do it. No matter how fucked up my life is, I'll have the baby and make it work somehow. I wonder how selfish that is. And Dom has to be told. The – foetus? – is in my body, but it's his child as much as mine. And then what will happen between me and Erazmus?

I want everything sorted out as soon as possible. I consider letting my family know before anyone else, because Mum will be brilliant and supportive, but it's only right to tell Dom first; I feel guilty for having been unable to keep it from Erazmus.

I let Dom wrap his leg around mine under the dining room table and tolerate him brushing my arm as we eat our meal. I smile at him, and his gaze softens, quashing my fears, and suddenly I feel confident about telling him the news. I have no idea how he'll take it, but it's my duty to let him know. After dinner I go outside as usual for a cigarette, and as usual, Dom follows me. Lydia, who hadn't been at dinner, is sitting on one of the chairs, hunched over so her head's nearly touching her knees. Her eyes are red and puffy, and it hits me that she's getting worse, not better. I get another wave of guilt. I haven't had a proper chat with her in weeks – partly because every time I turned around, Dom's there, and partly because I've been wrapped up in myself. I take the other chair, while Dom stands nearby, and I ask a stupid question. "Are you okay?"

Lydia arranges her mouth so it's in a straight line, tries to bring some warmth into her eyes, and says, "Fine," before stubbing her cigarette out and stalking back indoors. Dom, so oblivious to Lydia it makes me angry, pulls up the chair she'd been sitting on so our legs are touching. He smiles at me until I can't not smile back, and then, horrified, I drop my cigarette. A cider is one thing, but I shouldn't be smoking! Where's my head?! Dom's startled and asks me what's up. So I tell him. And, in a gesture that reminds me of Erazmus' the day we went to Tamehaven, Dom takes my face in his hands, looks into my eyes and says that he's so happy, that he loves me, and now we'll always be together. I'm relieved at his happiness, but being together is not what I had in mind. I smile and say I'm happy he's happy, but that I like him as a friend and don't want to get married. He seems not to know what I'm talking about, and says, "Of course we'll be together – we'll be a family." And then he tries to kiss me.

I panic. I don't know what to do. I jump off my chair, shouting "No!" and stumble back inside, pushing past Bonnie, who's finishing clearing up, and run up to my room. I lie on my bed and let my quilt soak up my tears. What had I been expecting? A few minutes later, there's a knock at my door. It's Bonnie.

"Can I come in?" she asks, as she slowly pushes open my door and crosses the carpet. I get up and throw myself into my chair by the window. I try to look out on the darkening garden. Bonnie lowers herself gingerly onto my bed and asks me what's up. The tears come again, and on autopilot I tell her I'm fine. She smiles and asks me why Dom's also upset. Apparently he'd started shouting and swearing and throwing himself about, and had chucked one of the chairs into the pond. Heather had to haul him inside and calm him down, which meant he got a diazepam and a drug-induced early night. I let out a sob, but that's all. Bonnie informs me that she's just going to sit on my bed until I tell her what's bothering me, and she says it with a good-natured smile, but adds that when it involves another resident, especially one as volatile as Dom, it had better be soon. I stare down at my hands, realising that I am out of options. Then the words tumble out.

I cry a lot and Bonnie puts her arms around me, telling me we'll get it sorted. I am so comforted and grateful that I even tell her I'd accidentally had a drag on a cigarette, and hope that I haven't damaged the baby. I want to tell her about Erazmus, too, but I hesitate, and in that instant she says, "You're only just pregnant though, Lizzie; we'll get it sorted." That kills the moment, snaps me back to my senses. I am alone again. I will always be alone. She's implying that I should have an abortion, but I haven't got the energy to argue with her, and turn my face away instead.

Eventually, Bonnie gets up and leaves, and I get ready for bed. On my desk, next to my face cream, is the receipt for the pregnancy test. I stick it on the wall with the rest of my clues to the meaning of the universe. As the last of the light fades away, I lie on my bed in my pyjamas and put my hand on my abdomen. I whisper *Twinkle, Twinkle, Little Star* because it's the only nursery rhyme I can remember.

Erazmus

Lizzie is pregnant by Dominic Whiley. I'll say it again, because I can't believe it – Lizzie is pregnant by Dominic Whiley. Stupid, stupid girl! And if she's stupid, what does that make me? Starting a relationship with a patient! A patient who's twenty years my junior. It could be the end of my career; if anyone recognised us in Tamehaven ... I don't know what's come over me. When I'm with her, I'm acting like I'm in love. Let's be accurate here – I'm acting like a young man in love for the first time. Do I actually love Lizzie? It's not like I know nothing about her – I know more about her than her own mother does! If this was happening to somebody else, I'd call it a midlife crisis exacerbated by a wife whose clock is ticking. Julia and I have been married for twenty years this September, and I have to keep reminding myself I loved her enough to marry her. It frustrates me beyond belief that I prepared her for this eventuality before I proposed – I wanted to be a professor, to excel in my field, to give something useful back to the world; I knew I would never want children. We'd discussed it countless times!

Should I stop working with Lizzie? We've come so far, and she's struggled so much with this that I don't want to desert her in the middle of her treatment. I want her to be okay. But is it love? I know she likes me; I think she loves me. Unless she's going through some weird Freudian phase and perceives me as a father figure. Should the fact that I'm asking myself these questions mean that I know the answers and don't want to face them? I'm a man in his mid-forties who's having a midlife crisis. Or is that explanation just a cop-out? If it's a midlife crisis, I don't have to change anything – just give my wife a child, forget about a pretty twenty-something patient, be content with my status as consultant psychiatrist, and wait for this phase to burn itself out.

Julia and I have barely spoken in days, but tonight she seems more like her usual self. She kissed me when I got home, and I can see that she's cleaned the house thoroughly. She says we're having steak for dinner, and I know she hates cooking steak because the fat spits everywhere. She hands me a glass of red wine, and tells me to go and change while she's cooking, which I duly do. Usually, I just take off my tie and my jumper, and roll up my shirt sleeves, but tonight I put on a pair of old jeans, and my faded AC/DC T-shirt. I go into the office Julia and I share, flip through my notes, and begin to draft my book. There are two people I need to include in it though – Lizzie and Dominic.

Which brings me back to square one. Lizzie can't go through with this pregnancy; she just can't. It's not sensible. Both she and Dominic are sick, neither is in any fit state to work, neither of them has their own home. And if anything were to ever happen between myself and Lizzie –the thought of Dominic coming round to take the child out for the weekend – the whole thing is ridiculous, and I'm livid that Lizzie could let something like this happen.

I feel more than anger, though, and that's the problem. Lizzie had sex with another man, after we had our time in Tamehaven – after we kissed. And, midlife crisis or not, that really, really hurts.

Lizzie

Who knows? Dom, Erazmus, Bonnie, Heather and my mum. I've begged Mum not to tell Dad or anyone yet. They all say I should have an abortion. After all, how can I hope to raise a child when most days I struggle to get up and about; when I've cleaned off a piece of broken glass and cut myself with it every night before I go to bed, like it's some kind of fucked-up prayer? I tell them all that I'd cope. Something inside me knows that when the baby comes, I'll be ready. Things will fall into place and I'll be okay. I'll be a mum – I will have fulfilled my biological purpose for being on the planet, and it will be okay. Erazmus will come round, I know he will. How could he not? Who doesn't feel complete, holding a baby? Dom will be okay – he'll recover. After all, he's at The Stables. If he was that bad, he'd still be in hospital. Erazmus and I have had a long chat about my medication, and we've decided that it would be potentially harmful for me if I came off them – to put it bluntly, if I make a suicide attempt, the baby will die. This baby will make everything be fine. I've thought of a better name for her if she's a girl – *Hope* - the last thing at the bottom of Pandora's box.

Erazmus

Sleeping in the spare room and avoiding Julia is not conducive to finding a solution. As evening falls, I pull out of Eskwich Hospital car park determined to have a proper, sensible conversation with Julia when I get home. We've reached an impasse: she's desperate to have a child; I feel the opposite. The cold realisation that this will end our marriage hits me.

I force myself into pragmatism. My book is writing itself, and I have no doubt that it will further the course of psychiatry in this country; in order to complete it, I need to focus, to rid myself of ridiculous distractions. I take what has been, until recently, my habitual way home – the most direct route – and my Mercedes is beside Julia's Audi in under five minutes. I refuse to hesitate in the car: I don't take a deep breath before I open the door; I don't head straight upstairs. I can hear Julia banging pans and cupboard doors in the kitchen; the aroma of her delicious spaghetti bolognaise fills the house.

"I know it's only a spag bol, but it smells divine," I say to the back of her head when I walk in. She turns towards me, pulling a bottle of red from the wine rack. She's on the verge of tears. "Julia," I murmur with an apologetic smile, and dropping my papers on the kitchen table, I move towards her, and hold her. She's rigid in my arms, but I can feel her trembling, so I draw her closer to me and stroke her hair. I've always marvelled at how soft it is. It smells of Vidal Sassoon Wash & Go. She mumbles something into my shoulder, but emotion cuts her off and she simply lets herself cry. I hold myself very still and continue stroking her hair, but I can feel salt water splashing onto the back of my hand.

Eventually the tears stop, and Julia bends down to fuss Fly, who's been purring and rubbing around our feet. She turns her face up to me with a weak smile. "He always knows when I'm upset," she says.

I return her smile, and move to the hob to rescue the bolognaise, while she takes two glasses from the cabinet and fills them with the wine. She hands one to me, and takes a long drink from hers, then puts the kettle on to boil, and reaches for the cylindrical spaghetti container. It's empty. I watch her pause in her fluid movements, then open the cupboard to take out the spare packet. She rifles around in the cupboard for a moment, closes it, rests both hands on the worktop, and drops her head. There's no spaghetti. I wait for the jerk in her shoulders which will tell me that she's crying again. It doesn't come. I sip my wine, place the glass on the table, and cross the kitchen. Julia had taken off her court shoes, but she's still wearing her work clothes. Nude tights, powder blue fitted shirt tucked into her black pencil skirt. Her posture pulls her shirt tight enough for me to see the outline of the white lace bra beneath. Her working day and my stroking has partially restored her blonde hair to its naturally wavy state. She's beautiful, and I love her. How can I tell her we needed to divorce? Resting my hand on her slender shoulder, I say, "It's okay – we'll have it with tagliatelle instead."

"We haven't got any fucking pasta! It's not going to work, Erazmus!" Julia smashes her hands onto the worktop and spins round to face me, knocking her wine glass over. We watch the red liquid spread, and drip over the side onto the floor, splashing up the kitchen cupboards as it makes contact. The glass rocks on the worktop. It isn't going to fall. Julia snatches it up and throws it onto the tiles.

Although I can hear Julia crying upstairs, I decide to walk the short distance to the corner shop and buy some spaghetti. Before leaving, I check the kitchen cupboards to see if there's anything else we're running out of, and in doing so, realise that I can't remember the last time Julia and I had done a food shop together; or when we last shared a meal. I realise I haven't been paying much attention to the state of the house at all. The fridge door has fingerprints on it, and some liquefying raspberries have fallen out of their plastic container and left vermillion stains on the shelves and on the bottom of the tub of butter. I wonder what the butter is doing on the shelf with the soft fruit. Taking a pen and a Post-it from their usual place on the kitchen side, I make a shopping list. I notice that our beautiful wooden table is covered in rings of coffee and tea, but when I look in the cupboard under the sink, the special wood polish we use isn't there. I add it to the list.

It's almost 9 p.m. before I carry our dinner and two more glasses of wine up to Julia. She's curled up against the headboard, flipping the pages of the free paper. She glances up, sighs, and folds the newspaper.

"Erazmus, this isn't working," she says.

"I know. But we need to eat." Placing the tray that holds our meal on the end of the bed, I climb up beside Julia. "Come on," I urge. "Eat." I hand her a fork, and she graces me with a flicker of a smile.

After a moment, she breaks the companionable silence. "You always did like your pasta al dente."

"Whilst you prefer yours to melt in the mouth," I counter, with a grin that immediately fades.

We sleep in the same room, and I hold Julia like I had when we'd been students. We lie very still. The sadness is absolute.

I'm still unutterably sad when I reach The Stables on Monday, but I press it down. I have to treat my patients. I have to end this insane situation with Lizzie. I harden myself, but, catching sight of my reflection in the dining room window as I pass, I allow myself a small smile. By the end of the day I'll be a free man again.

All is well at The Stables, under the circumstances. I'd prepared myself to speak at length with Heather about Lizzie's condition, but when we have our usual meeting in the dining room, she informs me that Lizzie had told her she's seen her doctor and has 'made the right decision'. This sounds ambiguous to me, and my concern must be evident, because Heather laughs and says, "Oh, Erazmus! She's having an abortion, of course!" Her relief is palpable and infectious.

"And Dominic?"

Heather gives a tight smile. "He's at The Bungalow for the time being. Dunstan's gone with him, and is staying in the other room." She pauses. I say nothing. "Lizzie told him about the baby. No one knows exactly what was said, but it's clear they will not be playing happy families. The problem I have now is that I have to find one of them another place to live."

I am dreading my session with Lizzie, but I have a duty of care to her. I also have a duty of care to me. Luckily, Lizzie is a person who is most healthy mentally when she's in flux and there is a crisis to sort out. She presents as calm, and slightly aloof. She looks older. She looks radiant. We discuss her condition, her plans, her mental state and her relationship with Dominic, as psychiatrist and patient. I hesitate, but only for a moment, before asking her if she would like to be assigned to another psychiatrist. She stares at me, all blue eyes and smoky make-up. "Why?"

I leave The Stables feeling incredibly relieved and incredibly lucky. If Lizzie had requested a different psychiatrist, everyone would have wanted to know why, and that could have jeopardised my career. We'd arranged to meet on my day off, just to talk things through properly somewhere we could be sure we wouldn't be overheard. Our session had concluded with platonic smiles.

As we'd arranged in our session, we meet in Tamehaven. I've taken the day off – I have to use my annual leave or lose it, and this year, because of my book, I've decided to use it. Lizzie's taken the train – partly so that she can show the ticket to the staff at The Stables, if they ask, and partly so no one will see her get into my car. If anyone does see us together, ostensibly we've just bumped into each other. I'm not prepared to jeopardise my career again. We'd planned to bump into each other by a bench on the promenade, and I stare at the ocean while I wait. It's still and flat as glass, reflecting the cloudless blue sky. Lizzie approaches from the town side. She looks happy. Her cheeks are flushed pink with the cold and her quick walk, and her blue eyes sparkle.

"Hell's bells!" She laughs and sits down, leaving a reasonable gap between us. "I didn't know you did casual!"

I laugh, and glance down at my battered old AC/DC T-shirt and jeans. "Well, you know, I didn't expect to see anyone I knew today," I say with a grin.

She asks me if I'd bought the T-shirt at a gig, so I tell her about when Julia and I had driven all the way to London in the brand-new white Ford Escort my parents had bought us as a wedding present; how we'd seen them at the Hammersmith Odeon, as it was then, and whereas I'd just been interested in seeing the Australian headliners, Julia had wanted to see Starfighters, who were supporting them. "She was always so much cooler than me," I say, smiling fondly at the memory. "She even wanted to call our cat 'Blues' after their song, *Alley Cat Blues,* but I won her over with 'Fly', after Marty McFly in *Back to the Future.*"

Wrapped in nostalgia, I forget myself, shift over to Lizzie, put my hand over hers and give it a little squeeze. "You're a bit of a rocker, aren't you? We should go to a gig together!"

When I turn to face her, Lizzie's eyes are burning into my skull.

"Who the fuck is Julia?"

I don't wear a wedding ring – I never have. Julia and her family baulked at it at first, but I said I didn't need a piece of jewellery to prove that I'm married. We made our vows in the sight of God, because that was important to Julia, and we signed the legal documents. Jewellery hampers your movements, harbours bacteria; and if it means anything to you, you spend every day afraid that you'll lose it. I gave them so many reasons that, ultimately, they accepted it. In

Lizzie's mind, though, it's no ring, no marriage.

She jumps up and turns on me like a cat. Time slows down and I watch us on the promenade, an observer; when I move, it's as if I'm wading through treacle.

Lizzie is screaming at me that I've lied to her, had a relationship with her under false pretences, abused my position, broken the law; that I've never had any intention of taking our relationship any further, that I've never had any intention of helping her raise her baby, that this is a game to me, that I'm just another bloke using her to get his kicks. I try to move closer to her, to hold her, to at least stop her yelling these things in public. She notices me glancing around for onlookers, and it throws petrol on her fire. A passer-by stops for a moment and stares at us, and instantly a gull spies its opportunity and dives in, knocking the man's fish and chips to the ground; immediately, a gang of other gulls and pigeons appear from nowhere, and there's noise and chaos as they scrabble for the scraps.

"I thought you had an abortion!" The words are out of my mouth before I know it. "I thought we were okay!" Lizzie freezes, staring at me in anguish and disbelief. I watch her heart break, and am rendered mute. Then she takes something out of her coat pocket, throws it at my chest and runs off. Stunned, I let her go. When she is out of sight, I crouch down and pick up the object she's thrown at me, which is now on the pavement under the bench. It's a plastic cactus, with a little tag attached to it, which reads: 'For your tissue table x'.

Lizzie

I've been used again. I can't believe that I've been used again. Especially by someone who is supposed to be helping me to recover. My grandfather had been dead for two years before I had the flashbacks – he got away with it. I refuse to let another man get away with treating me like this.

The Stables is a residential care home, not a hospital; I am allowed to shave my legs without supervision, and I am one of the lucky ones who can come and go as they please. This means that I can go to Tamehaven on the train, if I feel like it, and it means that I can make my way to my parents' house in Exeter, let myself in when I know they will both be at work, go into my old bedroom, and retrieve the five boxes of sertraline that I stashed away in the box of my old college stuff that I hid under my bed years ago, just in case. It means that I can come back to The Stables with a litre bottle of water, go up to my room, put *OK Computer* on repeat, and look out at the sloping garden and the greenhouse and the cold, blue sky while I write a letter to Heather, telling her what Dr Whittle has done to me, and declaring that my baby is actually his. If he can lie, so can I. *Let Down* comes on; my rage dissipates, and I start to cry. I allow the blackness to swallow me. I open the boxes and pop all the pills out of their blister packs. There is a fairly big pile on the floor in front of me. I am sitting cross-legged on the carpet, listening to Radiohead, watching the crows tumbling in the blue sky, and I grab a handful of pills, and swallow them with the water. I do it again and again, until there are no more pills. I do not allow myself to throw up. I stare at the sky, and I am shaking, and it is very cold, and I am dizzy. I find myself lying down, and I reach up to my bed to try and pull the duvet over me. I have lost hope. The last thing I remember thinking is, 'I have lost Hope.'

Erazmus

With a growl of frustration, I snatch the plastic cactus from where I've just placed it, on the top of the table, and slam it to the floor. After all these years, all that study, all that stress, all the sacrifices I've made and am still making; after all the good I've done, it took one sentence from one patient – one simple sentence – for them to suspend me with immediate effect. I can't believe it. And that jumped-up idiot, Sasha Grosvenor, has got his hands on the keys to my office before they've taken my ID pass from me!

As I glance into reception, my secretary, Linda, graces me with an expression I can only describe as regretful, before I am ushered out of the department. The heavy door buzzes and clicks locked behind me, leaving me on equal footing with those on the other side of this institutional relationship – the patients sitting on the moss-green upholstered chairs, waiting to be seen; confused and impotent, lacking agency and control. A young woman I have been treating for some time, Kayleigh, smiles at me through her mass of hair, rocking her new baby as she waits, oblivious to my predicament. She probably thinks that I've gone to complete some small but pressing errand before our appointment. Grosvenor will tell her that an illness has necessitated my immediate departure, and I am certain that he will discharge her, as she is no longer acute. A recently bereaved, new mother who has bipolar disorder, and no familial support. This, supposedly, is 'responding to the financial crisis in the NHS'. Whatever happened to 'prevention is better than cure'? It's a numbers game, and now, it seems, I am no longer one of their number. I shoot Kayleigh some kind of smile, and try to say it all with my eyes as I stride past.

"Dr Whittle."

I spin round, furious. "Yes, Dr Grosvenor?"

"You dropped something." The plastic cactus sits in his open hand; his eyes blaze with triumph.

The tyres screech as I swing my Mercedes out of the hospital car park. I'm not heading anywhere in particular; I just have to be emotionally, literally and legally, away from here. I command myself to calm down.

I cannot go home – Julia called in sick on Monday and hasn't gone back to work. She told me as I rushed out of the door this morning that she has an appointment with the doctor today. When I asked her what was wrong, she said that she feels 'a bit run down', which is vague, and no reason to be off work. She said it with a smile on her face. She is probably making preparations to leave me. I am sick of trying to second-guess her.

I find myself on the A380, and realise I am heading for Bishopsham. I have to see Lizzie. She might not even be there any more – they might have had her transferred to somewhere, or she might be with her parents – but that's where I have to start. I need to speak with Heather, as well. They can't possibly believe that I am the father of Lizzie's unborn child! It's farcical. It's just the bigwigs making a show of following a process – an allegation has been made, and they have to look into it. This is what I tell myself. I am a respected psychiatrist; Lizzie is a volatile girl whose mental illness is severe enough that she has been placed in residential care. I refuse to say the words that are lurking at the back of my mind: 'How could she do this to me?!' I take a deep breath and force anger down; music always helps, so I press the button for the CD player. *OK Computer* starts up. Immediately, I jab the button hard to turn it off, but it's too late – the tears are already stinging in my eyes.

At the top of the hill, I see the big, grey stone with 'The Stables' cut into it, and turn up the steep drive. The grounds really are very pretty; I make myself notice the yellowish catkins hanging from the trees, the succulent stalks of daffodils emerging from the dark earth. There isn't a car park at The Stables – you just arrive at the top of the drive and stop your car before you end up on the grass. I have never had trouble parking here. Until today. What on earth is going on?

I reverse back down the drive and look for a space on the street. There aren't any. This is ridiculous! I punch the steering wheel – my eyes are filling with salt water again. I am getting so worked up, going round and round the houses, that I admit defeat and drive back down into town, park in the multi-storey, and hike back up the hill. It is now nearly lunch time, and as I make my way to the front door, I expect to see everyone in the dining room, as I normally would. Hearing puffing, and quick footsteps behind me, I stop and turn my head. Dunstan squeezes past me with a grin and a flick of his eyebrows. "You're a dark horse, Erazmus," he says softly, "I didn't have you down as part of the club! You know she can't cook though!" He laughs and disappears through the front door.

Looking through the dining room window, I see Heather and virtually her entire team in there, and they are not eating – they are having a heated discussion. I pause, wondering what's going on, and where the residents are, and who is supervising them, when Heather looks up from some papers, straight into my eyes. Her gaze becomes a glare, and she jerks her head at me, in the direction of the front door, excuses herself, and leaves the room. I make a hasty attempt at smoothing my appearance, but Heather is already out of the front door and on the path before I've taken two steps towards it.

"Erazmus, I have to ask you to leave."

"Heather, what on earth is going on?" My tone is incredulous, but I am afraid, now.

"You can't be here, Erazmus," Heather reiterates.

In spite of knowing that in the light of the accusations, she is being the consummate professional. Heather's words and reactions hurt me. I take a couple of steps further towards her.

"Heather, please, you cannot possibly believe Lizzie's

story!" I counter. "This is ridiculous! I have been falsely accused, and wrongly suspended! You've known me for years – do you honestly think I'd involve myself with one of my patients?!"

Heather cuts me off before I can continue. "Erazmus, I honestly don't know what to think. One of the most reliable residents we've ever had doesn't come down for breakfast this morning, I send Bonnie up to check on her, there's no answer, we force the door, and Lizzie is unconscious on the floor, with empty blister packs, and blood everywhere. And then I find the letter she's addressed to me." She sighs, and her voice softens for a moment. "I really want to believe it's not true." She pauses. "I haven't forgotten the bonfire."

All I can say is, "What ..?" and I just stand there, in utter disbelief, while life as I've known it falls away.

"So as you can imagine, Erazmus, I have rather a lot on my plate at the moment, and I really think the best thing for you to do is to go home."

"Heather," I am almost whispering. "Is Lizzie ... ? Where is she ... ? What about ... ?"

"She's in hospital – I'm not going to tell you where – with serotonin syndrome. She miscarried."

Lizzie

I open my eyes, with difficulty – my eyelids feel really heavy – and immediately recognise a hospital ceiling. The adrenalin starts pumping, but I'm still a bit hazy and unsure as to what's happened. My eyes trace the curtains which are closed around my bed; the equipment I'm attached to. I try to work out what time and day it is, but it's too much effort, and I drift off again.

I can't believe it – I am back in AAU! Apparently, this one is in Exeter, but it could be anywhere – everything is beige; the pre-made tea is tepid; there's a grille on my door. I sit on a stool in a special room to take my meds, and they check in my mouth and under my tongue to make sure I've swallowed them. The mugs are plastic; there are no sharps.

I had a very long assessment with a lot of people, but I couldn't utter a word. In the end, they decided to leave me in the AAU. I have no idea whether I have been sectioned or not. I can't make sense of it, and nor, it seems, can the powers that be. At some point I have to see the police, but I can't face that yet, and the staff here are being very sympathetic. It is clear by the way they treat me that I am not just thought of as 'unwell' – I am also a victim.

They've tried to get me to talk about Erazmus and Dom and everything, but I can't. Heather has been in, as has Phee, and Bonnie, and they even got my mum to have a go. But I can't – I physically can't. I have another two labels that no one knows about: liar, and murderer.

I am mute until this girl called Kayleigh arrives. She's really nice – she's kind and friendly, and always gets me a cup of tea if she goes to get one for herself. She even picks the snails up when they come onto the path and puts them back in the garden so they won't get eaten or stepped on. After few days of smiling at each other when we pass in the corridors or in the garden, she comes and sits next to me on the sunny bit of a bench one day, and offers me a cigarette.

On reflex, I start to say, "Thanks, but I can't – I'm pregnant," but stop myself after "Thanks", and take the rollie she's made for me. And then I can no longer pretend to myself that I have forgotten. I take a long drag on the rollie, and bite my lip to get control of myself. But Kayleigh starts crying before I do, telling me that they're going to take her little boy away, when she hasn't done anything wrong. I don't know what to do, so I just touch her shoulder, and listen. She says that she's bipolar, that someone set her up, and that the psychiatrist she'd been seeing for years suddenly went away, and some 'posh new boy in a waistcoat' gave the final order for her to be sectioned. Something clicks, and I ask her the name of her old psychiatrist. And then I really start listening to what she's saying.

When she finishes her horror story, she asks me how I ended up here.

I think about all the ways I could reply, but stammer out, "I ODd. Again." I don't need to say any more, and Kayleigh just smiles in sympathy. And then I go and get us some tea, and we have another rollie each, and just sit there until the sun goes down, sometimes chatting, sometimes silent.

The days pass. I eat my dinner like a good girl; watch some telly, like a good girl; have a little joke with the nurses when I'm taking my meds, like a good girl; and then I go to bed, like a good girl. One of the nurses calls after me, "Goodnight, Lizzie. Sleep well. And don't worry, love, I'm sure you won't be here long."

She's right – I won't.

Erazmus

I am an intelligent man. Maybe I'm a little narcissistic; but I honestly thought that I was above fucking up my life in the way that so many people do. I've kept myself under control at all times; considered the possible repercussions of everything I say and do before I say or do it. I could easily have married Julia within a couple of weeks of meeting her, but I wanted to make sure I knew what I was doing, what was important to me; I weighed up what I would and wouldn't realistically be able to sacrifice in my life, and then gave Julia opportunity after opportunity to end our relationship – I repeatedly told her what she could expect from a life married to me – and I remember clear as crystal what she said: "I love you, Erazmus – I would never hold you back."

I tried to make the best of a difficult situation. I could have walked out a thousand times, and with good grounds: she broke her vow to me. Not her wedding day vow – one more important than that – the vow that she would never hold me back. That was more important to me than anything she did 'in the sight of God'.

I could go on and on with instances of where I've bitten my tongue, actively calmed myself down, 'turned the other cheek', to do the right thing. Even the parties I missed out on when I was at university because I knew that if I was going to succeed, I needed to study; all the times where I've really needed a drink, or something stronger, but have abstained. Julia was always the cool one, the wild one, not me. Then I meet Lizzie Rowe, and it all goes out of the window; and as if that wasn't bad enough, my world comes crashing down because of a momentary lapse in concentration. I have even laughed at the irony.

And for the simple fact that I choose not to wear a wedding ring, a patient – a young mother – has been detained under a section, and her child has been removed from her; the woman I thought I was in love with has attempted suicide, and may well still die, and the foetus in her womb has died. This is all horrible, but on top of it, is the injustice – Lizzie said the baby was mine. The baby could never have been mine, because we never had sex. No one believes me.

When my hands thump the steering wheel, I realise that I am driving – very quickly – back up the M5. My damned rationality kicks in, and I am aware that I am a danger to myself and to other drivers in this frame of mind, so when I reach junction 30, I pull off and head for the services.

The air is thick with what Devonians call 'mizzle'. I am painfully cold, and my shirt is soaked through by the time I traverse the extensive car park and find the entrance. I stop just inside the doors and let the thin jet from the overhead heater warm me for a second while I wipe the droplets from my glasses, but someone shoves me and growls at me to 'get out of the fucking doorway'. I mumble an apology and take as many steps forward as I dare without my glasses on, still rubbing the lenses. I feel out of control.

I walk past the franchise coffee shops and restaurants, and sit on a chair in the massive general restaurant. The chair is pale and shiny – I'm unsure as to whether it is made of plastic or wood. A middle-aged waitress in shapeless, faded black trousers, with an apron tied around her waist, comes over and wipes the sticky table on which I have been leaning my elbows.

"You can't just sit here, you know," she says, flatly.

"I'm sorry?"

"You haven't bought anything, and you've been sat here for ages. The boss'll come and turf you out in a minute." She is glaring at me. I wonder if she thinks I'm homeless or have been kicked out by my wife for having an affair – a laugh escapes me, as the latter isn't far from the truth.

"Oh, I see. I'll have a large filter coffee, please …".

The woman laughs hollowly. "This isn't the bloody Ritz,

you know," she says. "You get a tray, pick what you want, pay for it at the tills there" She points across the blandly-decorated room to where three bored-looking cashiers are sitting with nothing to do. "And *then* you find a table." She stalks off a few paces, and I hear her mumble, "I'm not a bloody slave! Yuppy twat."

I look around the soulless space – there are more empty tables than I can be bothered to count – stand up, and move towards the drinks machine, stepping on a cold chip that someone else dropped hours ago. I squash it into the dark blue carpet.

Back at my table, I sip my scalding coffee, burning my lips and tongue, but it clears my mind. In that instant, it occurs to me that this must be how my self-harming patients feel – the pain clarifies.

I look at my watch and estimate that I have been here for an hour and a half. I need to consider my options and formulate a plan of action. I need to appeal against the decision to suspend me – I have to – I have worked damned hard to get to where I am, and I will not allow a stupid mistake to ruin my career. I recognise that this means I will have to lie, and that Lizzie could suffer more as a consequence. I remind myself that I am contributing to society; Lizzie is sponging off it. I need to tell Julia something. I need to go home, arrange my affairs, and make myself presentable. I need to push down the urge to try to release Lizzie. What will I do, run away to Greece with her, open a cafe on the beach and live happily ever after with her and little Dominic Junior?

Draining the cold dregs of my coffee, I stand up and walk purposefully out of the restaurant. I pass the woman who is not a slave, force a smile and thank her for her hospitality.

But when I pull out of the slip lane and back onto the motorway, tears are streaming down my cheeks. Again.

Lizzie

This is the worst night of my life. I have no pills and no alcohol, and I can't scream, or cry too loudly, because they won't let me out otherwise. I am thinking about my baby; Hope if she was a girl, or Matthan for a boy. I will never know. No one knows. Except maybe God, if he's up there. I am thinking about Dom, and wondering whether they have told him that his baby is dead – and I wonder how he's going to feel about it, about me. I am thinking about my parents, with me in hospital again, that I tried to kill myself – again – which is bad enough in itself, but that in doing so I robbed them of their unborn grandchild. I am thinking about Kayleigh, and her living baby son, Liam, and how they need Dr Whittle. And I am thinking about Dr Whittle, Erazmus. I shouldn't have lied; but he broke my heart! I am torn between feeling glad that he's been punished for what he did, and guilty because he's probably lost his job and his wife and his home, and oh my God – what if he has kids?

I do not sleep. I writhe and cry under my blankets, and when it gets light, I find the kind nurse and tell her I made it all up. She goes to tell her boss. I go into the garden. Kayleigh is there. She's just rolled a cigarette, and she passes it to me, saying, "You look like you could do with one!" I take a couple of drags. How can I kill myself here? I know I don't have much time. I do the only thing I can think of – I run at the fence and start to climb.

Erazmus

By the time I turn off the main road through our housing estate, and onto the herringbone-paving of our cul-de-sac, I am calm, and rational. Even the unexpected sight of Julia's Audi on the drive doesn't faze me.

I park parallel to Julia's car on our double drive, although I reverse in, as is my habit. Her car is pristine, though sparkling with tiny rain drops, and as I walk past it to get to our front door, I note that there is nothing left on the seats – as is her habit. When I exit my car, I always have to shuffle through the pile of admin and books that lives on my passenger seat, so that I can bring in what I intend to work on during the evening; there are pens and CDs in the door compartments, and I usually have a spare shirt, and my newspaper in the back – there are signs of life. I think Julia must have her car valeted every couple of days; there's never even a hair, or a speck of dust on the dashboard.

I turn my key in the lock and shout a cheery "Hello" as I walk in, immediately aware that I am overcompensating. I drop my papers onto the kitchen table – Julia is not there. I fill the kettle and switch it on to boil – I could really do with a large glass of red, but I need to stay in control. I take my mug and Julia's cup out of the dishwasher, and pour the hot water into the cafetiere, along with five heaped scoops of fresh Colombian coffee. We keep the coffee in the fridge – the packet sealed with an oversized paperclip. I expected Julia to have come and joined me – and it's then that I notice the sound of the shower running. I would have had one myself, if she hadn't been in, and am a little annoyed that the bathroom is occupied – despite having the car heater on all the way home, I haven't been able to warm up since getting drenched earlier, and the cavernous restaurant in the service station did nothing to help. I wonder if Julia had told me that she had an aerobics class today – I am acutely aware that I haven't really taken notice of the day-to-day conversations we've had for quite some time. But how long? Since I met Lizzie? Since I started my book? Since we got Fly? Since we returned from our honeymoon? Guilt hits me like a tonne of bricks.

I sit at the kitchen table, trying to act normally. I sip my coffee and peruse the newspaper. I'm intending to work on my book later, and keep looking over at the folders that I've left on the end of the table.

Eventually, Julia enters the kitchen. She is wearing the dusky pink silk pyjamas that I gave her on her birthday, fluffy socks, and her hair is wrapped in a towel. She is devoid of make-up, and my face relaxes into a genuine smile. She looks so pretty, so vulnerable.

She is surprised to see me. "Oh. Hello. You're home early," she says, and walks up to accept the cup of coffee I pour for her. Her perfume is heady – *Obsession*, it's called. I secretly laugh at that irony, too.

"Yes, my last patient couldn't attend her appointment, and I thought I'd come home and cook you dinner …"

"And work on your book." She follows my gaze to the files on the end of the table, but she says it with a smile, so I give an apologetic one in return.

"Aerobics?" I ask.

"Yes," she replies. She has already finished her coffee, but I'm not surprised – it must have been tepid at best. She wafts past me, and I am almost sedated by the heaviness of her perfume. She reaches down, takes a bottle of red from the wine rack, and pops it in the fridge. "Just for ten minutes – it's better slightly chilled," she says, reading my expression. "How about a glass now, and I'll order a chinese instead?"

We talk in the kitchen for a long time, and the bottle of Beaujolais Village has gone before our food arrives. I feel as if I am falling – when did we last have a takeaway? I know I've drunk more wine than I should have. We're talking about our plans for our futures like we haven't since we were students, and it's lovely, but there's something off-kilter about it. I presume it's my brain's way of coping with what has happened today, and I decline when Julia suggests opening another bottle, put my glass in the dishwasher, and pour myself a large glass of water. "Spoilsport!" she teases, but follows my lead.

"Julia, I've decided to take the next couple of weeks off so that I can concentrate on my book," I tell her, keeping my voice level.

"Oh," she says, and sits on the chair next to me. "You'll be using the office here, then?"

I nod, but don't process what she's said: I have to get my story out before I forget it. I continue, "Sasha – Sasha Grosvenor, you remember him, don't you? – he's up to speed with my patients – he's been shadowing me for months – there's never going to be a better time, and the book isn't going to write itself!" I pause. "In fact, I was thinking about taking a sabbatical."

"A sabbatical?" she echoes. "What sort of sabbatical? Are you going abroad? Are you leaving me right now? I mean, I know we've talked about our plans, but they're just plans – I …" She stops to gain control of her wobbling mouth, and blink back the salt water that's threatening to spill from her eyes. "I was rather hoping this would take longer, that maybe having a little time apart would," Julia realises that the ending to her sentence is ridiculous, but she can't stop now she's started, "would bring us back together." The tears course down her naked face, while I sit there, staring at her. In seconds, she is bent double in the kitchen chair, sobbing.

"Look, Julia, we haven't had an easy time of it lately, but we have talked – we just talked – and we know we can't continue together when we disagree on something as major as having children. But we can't be in limbo forever, and, as I just said, there is never going to be a right time, and life can and does go on. You were always the creative one. You will be okay." I rub her back, and the towel slips off her head and falls between my feet. I try to run my fingers through her hair, but it's damp and not brushed, so I end up stroking it instead, which doesn't feel tender enough, so I cup her face in my hands and lift her head up. Her face is red, puffy and wet. I smile at her, fondly, and realise that is all I feel for her now – fondness. She has had too much wine; that's where the tears have come from.

She manages a smile, so I continue. "Taking a sabbatical – it's an idea I had today, and, to my mind, the timing is perfect, so I thought I'd discuss it with you before I set it in motion. I need some time and space to work on my book – you know that my goal has always been emeritus professor, and I'm in my forties now – we're not getting any younger!" I regret the words while I'm uttering them.

Julia snaps – snarling at me, suddenly on her feet. "'Not getting any younger'?! I know we're not getting any bloody younger! I know it better than you! I haven't got time to start another relationship, fall in love and hope it will be secure enough to raise a family! My body will *stop working* soon, and there is nothing – *nothing* – that I can do about it! I pinned all my hopes on you, Erazmus, and now you're fucking off to write your book, while I'm left here, on my own, stuck in a job looking after other people's children, to keep this roof over my head until you come back …".

"Julia, calm down. You've had too much wine."

"Well, you're having a fucking midlife crisis!"

"I explained to you, time and time again before we got married, that children weren't ever going to be on the agenda for me – I asked you to seriously consider before accepting my proposal, and you said, time and time again, that you loved me and would never hold me back."

"'Hold you back'?! Is that what children are to you? Obstacles?!"

"But you said …".

"I know what I said, Erazmus, but people – most people – *normal people* – change their minds as they get older! Why do you think I wanted to be a teacher? I've *surrounded* myself with children, Erazmus; you *can't* have not noticed how important they are to me! I've been a good little wife

76

and kept everything running behind the scenes while you go off every day and play the eminent psychiatrist – and I did it because I knew how important that is to *you*. I never held you back! I – stupidly, as it turns out – thought that when people love each other, they *compromise*. Look at everything I've sacrificed for you! I was sure – I'm *still* sure – that when your child is born you will love it and laugh at yourself for being so silly all these years. How can anyone not want a child! Life is a *gift* – it's our duty to share it! We would have been *good* parents, Erazmus; we would have raised a good child who would help the world in his or her generation. It's legacy. It's biology! It's what keeps life interesting – it's what keeps life *evolving!* Change *is* life! I'm a *human being*, for fuck's sake, not a fucking robot, like you! God! Sometimes I look at you, and I wonder what planet you're from! And you've built a career in *psychiatry*! Maybe it's *because* you're a psychiatrist! Look at you! You're not even angry – standing there stock-still with your head on the side like a fucking alien! You're analysing me, aren't you? You're fucking *assessing* me!" She pauses, then throws her hands in the air and storms out of the kitchen. I hear angry footsteps thudding up the stairs, and then the bedroom door slams.

I don't move. I feel cold. My mind is quiet and still. I listen to the clock ticking on the wall opposite the window. I count ten seconds, ten times, then scoop up my papers, wallet and car keys, and leave the house.

Lizzie

My hands are stinging. When I try to rub them, my movement is restricted, and I realise that they are bandaged. I find that I am lying on my back in a hospital bed. I have no idea where I am, or what day it is. I am still for a blessed moment. Then the anxiety kicks in; I become aware of my heartbeat, then that it is speeding up; then my mind is besieged. I remember the reasons for my actions, before I remember what I actually did. There is a yowl, like an animal in pain, and the face of a nurse fills my field of vision. Her mouth is moving, and her eyes are pleading, but I can't hear what she's saying. My limbs struggle against the tightness of the bed sheets – I have almost been swaddled! I am out of breath, and the noise stops. The sound had been coming from me.

They try to get me to eat, but the thought of it makes me gag. They try to prop me up on some pillows, but I slide back down until I am horizontal again and turn my face away. I keep my eyes shut. I am unable to speak.

Erazmus

I drive to Swansburne on autopilot. Darkness has fallen, and it's hammering down with rain. Spray from the vehicles in front splatters my windscreen, the wine I've consumed fogs my senses, and I'm dazzled by the headlights of oncoming vehicles. I know I shouldn't be driving.

I need to find somewhere to spend the night, and the only place I can think of is the bed and breakfast in the building with the turrets, on the seafront. I swing my car onto Marine Parade and am relieved to see that the laminated sign propped in the window reads 'Vacancies'. When I switch off the engine, I can feel the wind buffeting the car. I'm going to get cold and soaked again walking the fifty or so yards to the building, and curse myself for leaving without a jacket. The only clothing I have with me is the spare shirt that hangs in the back of my car. I hope that there'll be complimentary toiletries.

I hurry up to the hostelry with my head down, in a futile attempt to prevent the rain from getting on my glasses. The entrance to the building is a cheap, PVC door which swings too easily to be secure. There's no one behind the narrow reception desk, so I press the tarnished bell on the counter. It's not cold in here, but it isn't as warm as I'd hoped.

A woman with grey, permed hair and a baggy, woollen jumper shuffles up behind the desk. She's holding a cup of tea and is clearly surprised to see me – anyone – in her reception, at this hour, on a weekday night; but she smiles at me and gives me a room, commenting that she's just about to lock up. Taking in the state of me, she says she'll make me a cup of tea and bring it to my room. She's gone before I can thank her, or ask for coffee instead.

My room is on the ground floor, which is disappointing. I'm even more disappointed to find that there isn't so much as a bar of soap in the bathroom. I consider driving to the petrol station at the top of the hill to see if I can get anything there, but I'm suddenly exhausted. The landlady knocks softly on my door, and hands me a tray with a teapot, a jug of milk and a cup that wouldn't have looked out of place in my grandmother's house. I smile and thank her. I can't stand tea, but at least it warms me up. Then I stand, head down in the shower under scalding water for as long as I can bear it. I dry myself with a scratchy blue hand towel, put my socks and underpants back on, get into bed, and pull the sheets up over my head.

Sunlight streaming in through the thin, yellow curtains wakes me. I wonder where I am, but only for an instant. My first thoughts are of Lizzie – how must she feel, waking up in hospital? Will she even know what town she's in? Will she even care? I'm tangled up in the sheets, and they're damp in places, so I presume I've had nightmares, although I can't remember them. I'm warm enough, though, and safe – no one knows where I am – but I don't relish the prospect of getting up, being unable to wash properly, and putting yesterday's clothes back on. I scrabble around on the unfamiliar bedside table for my watch, and am shocked to find that it's after eight o'clock. I hurriedly dress in my still damp clothes, splash my face with water and try to tame my hair, before heading to reception. The landlady is at her post, with another cup of tea, flipping through the *Swansburne Gazette*.

"Good morning," I say, startling her. She looks up and smiles.

"Morning!" she says, brightly. "Did you sleep well?"

"Yes, thank you. I was wondering if I have time to nip out and get some shopping before you finish serving breakfast …".

The landlady laughs, displaying uneven, discoloured teeth. "You're our only guest, Mr …" She checks the thick black diary next to the bell. "Mr Whittle. You can have breakfast whenever you like!"

As soon as I step outside, I can taste the salt in the air. The sea is turbulent and grey; it booms against the wall which protects the town and the railway line from the waves, and I am surprised that I didn't hear it in the night. Julia would have loved that – she would have found it romantic. Lizzie would have, too. It occurs to me, not for the first time, that there are many similarities between them. I shake my head clear and pull myself together: neither of them had been there, and I hadn't heard anything myself. It's moot.

Instead of heading up to the High Street, I walk the short distance down to the sea. There is no direct access from Marine Parade – the raised and fenced railway line blocks the way – you can either walk towards Cardinal's Cove and the cliffs, and cross the line via an iron bridge, or you can take the route I choose: towards the railway station. A pretty, or picturesque, or twee – depending on your point of view – stream runs through the centre of Swansburne, which is famed for its black swans, and wildfowl enclosure. It flows straight down to the sea, so the railway line is carried over it via a double-arched stone bridge. I walk under just as an express train rattles through, and though the noise startles me, the pigeons that use the underside of the bridge as a roost don't bat an eyelid. I'd hoped I'd be able to traverse the seawall; however, the waves are crashing up and high over it, hitting the trains as they speed through, so I reconsider – I'm cold in my dirty shirt as it is – and stand hugging myself on the concrete, as close to the edge as I dare. The cold sea water stings my face. I lick the salt from my lips, turn around, cross the road, and make my way up the path that runs along the stream.

Hundreds of gulls are tearing across the leaden sky, with a cacophony of cries. On the water near the beach, two black swans and a few mallards bob about; the rest of the birds are further inland, on the banks and in the park. I wonder who gave the go-ahead for the planting of palm trees – Swansburne is the epitome of an English seaside town, and the palms are incongruous with the junk souvenir shops and the vulgar amusement arcade.

Passing the crazy golf course, I catch myself in the middle of a ridiculous daydream about playing a game with Lizzie and Dominic Junior, for his fifth birthday, or something; mock shaking hands at the end of the game, which leads to a passionate embrace, and then we walk over to the arcade, arms around each other, little Dominic running on ahead to go on the Thomas the Tank Engine ride, and after that I win Lizzie a cuddly toy from those grabbing machines, and buy us all an ice cream with a Flake in it. When I catch myself, I am amazed that it was Lizzie and Dominic Junior who popped into my head, not Julia and Erazmus Junior. Maybe it's because Dominic Junior was actually a possibility, where Erazmus Junior never was. I wonder what Freud would have made of it.

Pulling myself together for the umpteenth time this morning, I cross the soggy grass of the park, climb the steps to the through-road, wait for the rush-hour traffic to slow enough for me to wind my way between the cars, and go into Boots. The strip heater above the doors blasts me, and I become aware of how cold I am. I purchase my toiletries – I have an irrational urge to buy different brands, but I resist – and a set of novelty Easter socks and pants, then make my way to the little shop that sells wide-legged jeans and cheap sweatshirts to middle-aged men, and hurry back to the bed and breakfast, grabbing my spare shirt from the car before I go inside.

After another scalding shower – this time with soap and shampoo – a shave, and in clean clothes, I feel more like myself; I even take my notes for my book into the dining room. I love my work, and am quickly absorbed in my case studies. I lose myself – or find myself – I'm not sure which is closest to the truth – in it, and don't register the landlady's presence at my table until she places a claw-like hand on my shoulder. She startles me, but this time I am brave enough to request coffee instead of tea, and ask her name. Grace brings a cafetiere and this morning's copy of *The Guardian*. She presents it to me with a wry smile, and I tilt my head in puzzlement, to which she says, "You can tell a leftie a mile off!" She pauses at my table, but I prevaricate with asking her to join me, so she nods and shuffles off, chuckling.

When I next glance at my watch it is half past ten. I really need to get to my computer to type things up, but I can't go home, and I am hit by the memory that I can't go to my office any more, either. It is not my office now – it is Grosvenor's. I briefly wonder what changes he's made to it; in the next breath, I am furious with Lizzie. Finally, I am livid at myself. I am the architect of my destiny – it's nobody's fault but mine. The Led Zeppelin song plays in my head, and I wince at the memory of playing *Presence* in my car with Lizzie. Then panic grips me. I hastily gather my things, and go to find Grace, who is hoovering the hall carpet. She tells me that I am welcome to stay for a fortnight if I like, as the room isn't booked again until then; and suggests that I go to the library and use a public computer to do my work. She then apologises for calling me 'Mr' Whittle instead of Dr Whittle, and proceeds to question me about arthritis, to which I have to explain that I am not that kind of doctor. I cannot determine if she is disappointed, or impressed. I thank her, and book the room for exactly two weeks, and then head back out into the cold to find the library.

Julia

I am torn. I fully appreciate that my wanting a child is frustrating for Erazmus; at the same time, I am utterly heartbroken.

A decade his junior, when we married, I completely understood – or thought I did – that he didn't want children, and that his career was paramount to him. He was always passionate about his work, and I loved him for that – it was one of the things that drew me to him. And I was young – I was enjoying university, and excited about my own future. I'd seen my school friends have children early, and watched them dissolve into motherhood, and I really didn't want that for myself. Yet. I thought I felt as Erazmus did – I wanted to give something different, and more meaningful, back to the human race: *anyone* could have a baby – there was nothing special about that.

Except as I grew older, and as I worked with other people's children, I began to comprehend that there was nothing more special than having a child – nothing at all – to the point where my life seemed pointless without one. And now I have reached the point where my life *is* pointless without one, and – I hate the phrase, but I can't find a better one – my body clock is ticking. With every passing day, I am closer to the menopause, and dying childless.

When I was young, children were just noisy, messy burdens to be endured until they left home. At the end of my first semester at uni, I came home, and went out in the evening with a group of my girlfriends from school. Even my close friend, Shirley, had begged her mum to babysit for her so she could have a rare night out. Shirley had always enjoyed a few glasses of wine, but that night she virtually downed an entire bottle before we'd been in the pub an hour. Before long, she was a blubbing mess of snot and eyeliner, clinging onto my shoulder, venting exhaustion, anger, and frustration, along with her fears that she wasn't a good mother, wasn't cut out for it, couldn't cope with it, wouldn't be able to give her son a good enough life. Of course, I didn't have a clue what she was experiencing, and just wiped her face for her, and put my arms around her. Eventually I'd drunk more than I should have too, and I lost patience with her, and told her to go home. I vowed that would never happen to me. But the next morning, it occurred to me that she was experiencing something profound; it was hard sometimes, yes, but it was at the core of our biology. I thought about the things I'd learned at Sunday school.

And yet, here I am, approaching forty years of age; wondering who I actually married. If he cares so much for people that he dedicates his entire life to helping them through the darkest of times, how can he possibly not want to have children of his own? I don't understand him, and I don't know if I am sad or disgusted by that. Another cliché pops into my head: my husband doesn't understand me.

For all my reasoning, I couldn't get away from the fact that Erazmus was right – I had drunk too much wine last night, and after the anger has dissipated a little, the hangover kicks in. I lay as I am, sprawled across the double bed, with the foul taste of stale wine and sleep in my mouth, then realise that I have to get up for work. In the shower, I curse myself for getting carried away, on what Shirley jokes is a 'school night'. I try to justify it as some long-overdue venting, but I'm still cross.

When I am dressed and have put on my make-up, I stand still in the bedroom, realising that the house is unusually quiet. Erazmus isn't a loud person, but normally I would be hearing the kettle, or him emptying the dishwasher, or the sound of him typing in his office. Today there is nothing. It's a sad fact to have to admit to myself, but it's not unusual for Erazmus to sleep in the spare room; perhaps the wine has made him sleep in. I walk down the hall, but the door to the spare room is ajar – Erazmus isn't there, and instinct tells me that the bed has not been slept in.

I instinctively know that there will not be a note on the kitchen table, and that his car will not be parked next to mine on the drive. The central heating has already warmed up the house nicely, but I am suddenly cold all over, and I shiver.

Tears prick my eyes, but I blink them back. Erazmus is acting like a teenager, taking off in the middle of the night after an argument, but I now have to accept the fact that he isn't ever going to change his mind about having children; and although I find this cold, and selfish in the extreme, I have to accept that people are different, and he has a right to his opinion. And, though I am loath to admit it, he *did* talk to me at length about this issue before we got married – he was always open about it. I cringe as I realise that I am the one in the wrong here – I thought he'd change. No, be honest. I thought that if I 'accidentally' fell pregnant, he would change his mind. But I didn't get pregnant. Maybe there's something wrong with him. Maybe he knew, but he was embarrassed, and *that's* why he said he never wanted children. Maybe he desperately wants them but knows he can't have them – reverse psychology! Maybe I am clutching at straws.

Another thing he was right about is the fact that, no, we cannot go on as a couple, like this. A burning need to apologise overwhelms me, but I don't know where he is, and I have no way of contacting him. I have an irrational need for him to hold me and tell me everything is going to be okay. And it is too late for me to start again with another man. Maybe when Erazmus comes back I can apologise, accept my fate, be his wife again. As soon as this last thought flashes into my mind, I realise that all of this is ridiculous. I am wondering if I ever knew my husband, and that speaks volumes. If Erazmus has gone, then I am better off without him.

I make no further alterations to my routine, and when I step inside the staff room door, it's as if nothing has happened. I make a coffee, greet my colleagues, and go through my notes for today while I drink it. Then I go to my classroom, take the red plastic chairs off the tables, and attempt to write today's date on the whiteboard with an almost-dried-out marker pen. When the children enter, with their habitual cacophony, I am my usual, cheery self. But I make a mental note to book an appointment with the doctor.

Two days pass and Erazmus has not come home. I am now more worried about him than angry with him. It's all I can think about. At lunchtime, the head teacher, Mr Thomas – Mark – taps me on the shoulder as I stir my coffee. "That was quick!" he exclaims, and I am puzzled.

"Oh, hello, Mark! What was quick?" I reply.

"Oh." Now he seems puzzled. "Sorry, I thought I saw in the diary that you had a doctor's appointment in your lunch hour today – I must have been looking at the wrong page …"

"Oh my goodness. Thank you, Mark!" I gush. "Here, have a coffee – I'll be back as quickly as I can!" And I rush out to the car park, and drive as fast as I dare to the hospital.

I can't believe I'd forgotten about it! There was something I needed to find out, and in finding it out, I'd have to be brutally honest with myself. Erazmus and I had always enjoyed what I would consider a normal, active sex life. It was only when I started pushing the issue of children that we'd argued, and he'd felt more comfortable sleeping in the other room. Eventually I told him that I was going to stop taking my contraceptive pill, because taking it at my age was putting my health at risk. He was fuming – he'd never liked condoms – but he couldn't argue with the logic. I thought it would force the issue because I knew he wouldn't be able to keep his hands off me forever, and then when I became pregnant, he'd see it as fate, or at least admit his part in making it happen, and then paternal instincts would kick in, and he would be thrilled, and we'd all live happily ever after. The trouble was, I'd deceived him. I told him I was going to stop taking the pill – the truth was, I'd already stopped taking it. About eighteen months ago.

A few days later, Dr Farefield calls me back to discuss the results of the tests I'd had. My doctor's surgery is built onto the side of Eskwich Hospital – the hospital that houses Erazmus' department. As I make my way back to my car, his colleague, Sasha Grosvenor, strides out through the automatic doors. We don't know each other that well, but I call out to him before I realise I'm doing it. He spins round, and I wave. He must have been lost in thought, unless the drizzle had coated his glasses, because it takes a few seconds for him to realise who I am, give a little nod, and quickly cross the road to where I stand.

"Hello, Julia! How lovely to see you!" he says, genuinely glad to have bumped into me.

"It's good to see you, too Sasha," I return, almost asking him if Erazmus has made it into work, before remembering that he'd said he'd taken two weeks off. "You're looking well," I add with a smile. I mean it.

"As are you, Julia!" he replies. "In fact, you look like the cat that got the cream!" He pauses for a moment, and then asks, "I'm just going out for a bite to eat – if you're free, would you care to join me?" I'd just used the public phone in the hospital to call Mark and tell him that I won't be in for the rest of the day, overwhelmed as I am by my results. I know I will not be able to concentrate on the children; if I want a family, it is the end for me and Erazmus. That's my choice. This is the end of the Julia I know. So, on a whim, I accept Sasha's offer.

Sasha never goes unnoticed in a crowd, and everything about him – from the way he always dresses in a suit with a waistcoat, to the way he walks (it wouldn't surprise me if he had been a sergeant major before trying his hand at psychiatry) to his car (a Jaguar, of course) – says 'I am successful, I am in control, I get what I want'. Honestly, it's very attractive. His Jaguar is spotless, and aside from his driving glasses and a copy of *The Times* which he sweeps from the passenger seat as I slide in, there's nothing personal in the vehicle. I like a clean car.

When he asks if there's anywhere in particular I'd like to

eat, I laugh, and tell him I don't mind – even the cafes in Eskwich are better than the staff room at work – at which he shakes his head and smiles, and drives us to the Heron – a pub on the outskirts of town.

On a summer's day, The Heron is a beautiful place to be – a low, thatched, white-painted building, set against a backdrop of wooded hills, on the banks of the River Exe. The river passes under an ancient bridge, widens, and tumbles over a series of small rapids before making its way on down to the sea at Exmouth. The pub's gardens and a shaded seating area run the length of the Heron, from the bridge to the end of the rapids, but as the river sits at the bottom of a kind of gorge, the place is pretty well protected from flooding. There is a resident heron, of course, which, today, reminds me of Sasha, standing tall and proud and still in the centre of the river, while the turbulent water bubbles by, and countless tourists point and take photos. To be honest, I've actually taken a photo of the bird – more than once.

Today, however, it's cold, and we don't sit outside. The trees' new, fresh leaves are nonetheless spectacular against the slate-grey sky, and the river, though it mirrors that grey, is dramatic and violent; it's loud even with all the doors and windows shut. It's also high enough for me to be a little nervous.

Sasha plucks a menu from its stand, and we make our way to the far front left of the bar area. We sit at a table for two – a round wooden table, with leather, low-backed bucket chairs – by the floor-to-ceiling window that runs the length of this side of the Heron. He passes the menu to me, announcing that he will be having the steak, before asking if I would care to share a bottle of red with him. I accept his offer and say that if the steak is good enough for him to order without perusing the menu, then I will have the same. This seems to please him.

After placing our order at the bar, Sasha returns with a bottle of one of the more expensive cabernet sauvignons and two sparkling glasses. Pouring my drink first, he comments, "I must say, Julia, you are coping admirably with this situation – if I hadn't myself been affected by the events of last week, I honestly wouldn't know that anything was amiss." He sits, and though he is filling his own glass, his gaze never leaves my eyes. "You look confused," he adds.

I give a small, hollow laugh. "Ah. Then this fortnight he suddenly takes off *is* the start of his sabbatical, and he *did* arrange it at the eleventh hour. Yes, I must say it did come as a bit of a shock – I'd imagined that if he ever took a sabbatical, it would be because we would be cruising the world together – not him going off somewhere to write another bloody book!" I blush when I realise I have sworn, but I can't describe how angry and disappointed I am. When I return my gaze to Sasha, I notice that he now looks confused.

"Sabbatical?" Sasha pauses, and I can see that he knows he has said something he shouldn't have to me. He shakes indecision away, and says, "Julia, your husband hasn't taken a sabbatical – he has been suspended."

This must be what it is like to be one of those unfortunate people who laugh at funerals. I find myself laughing for a moment. I open my mouth to tell Sasha that he must be mistaken, but his firm, yet compassionate expression assures me that what he has said is the truth. I don't move or say anything for what feels like several minutes. Then I shake my head clear. Erazmus is not the sort of person who gets suspended. There has been a mistake. I say as much to Sasha.

He gives me a tight, regretful smile.

"Okay," I say, "please tell me what it is that Erazmus is supposed to have done." Then I am horrified by the thought that my husband might have been distracted by our argument and misread something, or mis-prescribed a drug, and someone has died as a result. I cover my mouth with my hands, and tears prick behind my eyes – poor Erazmus! And I'd yelled at him for being selfish! No wonder he walked out! But these emotions are quashed and, in a matter of seconds, I have done a one-eighty.

Because what Sasha proceeds to tell me is *so* much worse.

Erazmus

The rain resumes within minutes, so I duck into a charity shop and rummage through the clothes racks for a jacket. The only thing I can find which is even tentatively suitable for purpose, is one of those anoraks with the fur-rimmed hood, from the 1980s. The waterproof material is a dark, petrol blue, while the lining is almost neon orange, and although I instantly hate it, I know it will keep me warm. I ask its price from the lady behind the makeshift cash desk, and I wait while she judges how much I can afford to pay. She chooses a number. "That'll be twelve pounds, please, sir." I give a small, tight smile, but hand over the money. It's for Oxfam, anyway.

Of all the towns I've ever visited, Swansburne has the simplest layout – the railway is the boundary between the town and the ocean; the stream divides the town. There are shops, cafes and pubs on both sides of the stream, and they follow its course up to the point where there is a bridge, and the water disappears underground. The library stands where the shops become houses. It is impossible to get lost here.

I am so glad to be in the warmth of the library, that I audibly sigh when the PVC door swings shut behind me. I take off my steamed-up glasses and wipe them, then ask the girl on the desk if I can use a computer. She asks me for my library membership card. I am embarrassed to inform her that I don't have one, so she registers me, and hands me a white card with the Devon Libraries logo on it. Thanking her, I locate the computers, and sit down. There are only five, and two of them are already taken; I presume the young lads who are typing with their index fingers are both college students. Just as the welcome screen demands my ID number, the librarian – I can see her badge now my glasses are dry – taps me on my shoulder and hands me a slip of paper, saying, 'Sorry, you'll need this number – I forgot to give it to you when you were at the desk!'

I type in the number – I can't touch-type, but I am considerably faster at it than the students – open a blank Word document, and take my notes out of the bag that had contained my 'new' jacket. They are a little damp at the edges, from carrying them close to my body as I strode along the street, but nothing is smudged. Then it hits me what I must look like – a dishevelled man in somebody else's old jacket, holding a well-used carrier bag, coming into the public library to shelter from the rain. I cringe at the mental image, spread my papers about, take my Parker pen out of my trouser pocket, and am, thankfully, quickly absorbed in my work. Parker! That's what my new jacket is – a parka. I smile, and continue typing.

I jump at a tap on my shoulder. It's the young librarian again. "Excuse me, sir, but your free hour is up. There's no one waiting to use the computer, so if you pay a pound, you can have another hour if you like."

"Oh, I'm so sorry. I didn't realise," I say, fumbling in my trouser pocket for a pound coin. Fortunately, I find one, and pass it to the librarian, with an apologetic smile. Then I notice her properly – short, dark hair, bright blue eyes, button nose, bird-like movements. She reminds me of Lizzie. I am hit with a desperation to contact her – Lizzie. "Are you all right, sir?" she asks. I pull myself together, and thank her, but tell her I need to go now. I tear a page out of my notebook and scrawl a message to Lizzie on it – if I can't see her in person, then surely someone will pass her a note – but whom? My heart sinks as I realise that I need to go back to Eskwich.

Julia

It is very tempting to stay and order another bottle, and I am only half-joking when I put it to Sasha. He returns to work, of course he does, but before he stands up, he reaches across the table, and briefly covers my hands – which are wrapped around my now-empty glass – with his own. "You can always call me, Julia," he says, his eyes large and hypnotic behind his thick lenses. He takes out an NHS business card, looks at it with amusement, and scrawls something on the front, and a telephone number on the back. "That's my home number," he says. I thank him and watch him leave. He traverses the room as if he owns it. I pick up the business card he's left. I hold the card between my thumb and forefinger and spin it. On the front, he's added the word 'consultant' above his profession, so the card now proclaims that he is the Consultant Psychiatrist. Erazmus is the consultant psychiatrist, isn't he? How much in the dark am I?

I stare at the river and watch the heron until my back begins to ache. I ask at the reception area at the end of the bar if I can phone for a taxi. The shy, young girl at the desk passes the phone over to my side of the counter, when her manager politely intervenes, informing me that Dr Grosvenor has arranged for there to be a taxi outside waiting for me, and that the bill has been paid. I'm a little taken aback, so I thank them, and leave the bar. Sure enough, at the end of the path that leads through the garden, there's a private cab, ready to take me home. The wind pushes me towards it, and the fresh, infant leaves wave crazily against the dark, brooding sky.

The entire journey home, I've been preparing myself for finding Erazmus there, or finding he's still absent. I know I'm at a crossroads in my life, and that I have to play this carefully; but as I can't make my mind up what to do, or even what outcome I want, I've opted for honesty – the problem is, what I feel shifts every few minutes. I'm actually relieved when the taxi pulls up outside our – my – house, and the black Mercedes still isn't there. Once inside, I let the wind slam the door closed, stride straight for the fridge, and pull out the bottle of wine I'd mistakenly left there the night before. Honestly, leaving red wine in the fridge! I take a wine glass from the dishwasher, give it a perfunctory dry with the tea towel, and pour myself a glass, drain it in three gulps, and pour another, larger, one.

I scour the house. There's no note anywhere, and no more of Erazmus' things are absent – he clearly hasn't been back. So where is he? For a second, I empathise with him – this is everything he's ever worked for, gone in an instant. Panic flashes through me. What if he'd raided a hospital medicine cabinet?! And then I shake my head and laugh at myself – Erazmus was – is! – a psychiatrist; not to mention the most coldly logical and self-controlled person I've ever met. He'd never get himself into a situation that ironic! And then I remember what he's done, and the joke is on me.

Except it isn't in the slightest bit funny. It's the worst thing in the world. Again, I wonder if I've ever really known the man I married, in spite of his relentless apparent transparency. I haven't just been betrayed – if 'just' can ever precede 'betray' – I've been betrayed and humiliated. Does he love me? Did he ever love me? Does he love *her?* Is he even capable of love? How could he do this to me?! I've been the model of the perfect wife! I am childless because of him! All that time I wasted, trying, hoping, eating healthily, not smoking, not drinking. Even all those times afterward, pretending I was having a wash, when out of sheer desperation, I was actually on my back with my legs up against the bathroom wall, in the ridiculous hopes that gravity would help me. How could he do this to me?! With a girl! With a patient! How could he ever have found one of his patients attractive?! They're messed up, lazy, self-pitying …
I sometimes catch myself thinking that he should just let

them get on with it and kill themselves, and then I remember that anger is easy and safe, and that the work Erazmus does is so very important – it saves lives, and not just those of the patient – and he's battled with the stigmas in society against the mentally ill. I end up cringing that I blanketed all those people as lazy and self-pitying.

And then I get hit with a series of questions: is it more sinister than that? Oh my God, does it turn him on? If they're "investigating the allegation", is he looking at prison? And` finally, how many times has he done it before?

I clean the house from top to bottom. I change the sheets and the towels. I wash my car and vacuum it. I have a scalding hot bath, wash my hair, and shave. I have to be clean, and I have to be moving. I go downstairs in a fresh pair of pyjamas and drink a pint of water. I think about having the house repainted and recarpeted. I think about burning it down. I think about cutting up Erazmus' suits, or stuffing all his possessions into bin liners, and throwing them out of the window and onto the lawn, to shame him. But I don't do any of those things. In defiance against the rush of adrenalin, I make myself walk slowly into the now spotless hall, to the telephone. I take out the card that Sasha gave me and dial his number.

He answers on the third ring. "Julia!" he says, sounding not quite as surprised as I thought he would. "I wasn't expecting to hear from you again today – is anything the matter?" I can hear classical music in the background, but I can't name the piece.

"Sasha, I'm sorry to call you so soon – and so late in the evening!" My calmness deserts me. "I just – Erazmus isn't back, and I ... well ... I wondered ... I just ... needed to talk to someone." I cringe at my words. I'd cringe if I'd said them to anyone, but I said them to a psychiatrist! I imagine a slow, thin, ironic grin spreading across his face. "Sasha, I do apologise. That came out wrong. I've had some wine – I ..."

He laughs. "Don't worry, Julia. Today has been a bit of a shock for you. I'm afraid I'm very busy at the moment; however, I don't have to be in the office until 11 o'clock tomorrow – perhaps you'd like to join me for coffee in the morning?"

The next morning I throw caution to the wind and call in sick. I've never done it before without actually being ill, but I do feel odd – shaky, anxious. And there is something about this man. Or do I really mean this situation? Shirley answers the phone. It's lovely having my best friend as a colleague, but in situations like this it's a little awkward. She knows something is up, in that way that best friends do, and she wants to help. Part of me wants to tell her, but I don't know where I stand in regard to what I can say about Erazmus. Is it still hush-hush? Or are people getting wind of it, and I should respond with 'no comment'? I'm surprised no one from The Meadows has contacted me, to be honest, but then when was the last time I checked the answerphone? I think of the pile of post I've just been kicking to the side when I enter the house. I need to ask Sasha about all this. I opt for a kind of honesty with my friend. "Oh, Shirley, I'm all over the place! I'm fluey, I'm nauseous, I can't eat, I can't concentrate … I just feel dreadful. We need to have a catch-up sometime, but right now, I just want to go back to bed!"

Shirley sympathises and tells me that I must talk to her more. Then she redundantly, but automatically, covers the mouthpiece with her hand, and I hear her speaking in the hushed tones receptionists use when they're asking their boss if he wants to take the call, or if they should say he's 'presently unavailable'.

"Hello, Julia," Mark says brightly. "Look, you take as much time off as you need – I know you've been for tests. I'll cover your classes today – it's not a problem – and I'll get a supply in for the rest of the week, but, obviously, let me know where we stand as soon as you can, okay? Take care of yourself, Julia, speak soon." And he's gone. I have a week off.

A little disappointed that I won't see his home, I arrive early to meet Sasha in the Mad Hatters Cafe in Eskwich. He says he 'frequents' this place primarily because of its name, but they do no-nonsense food, and he drinks so much coffee, the owners let him sit there working for as long as he likes. I've never been there before – it's not my sort of place, and I'm surprised that Sasha goes there at all. I imagine him, in his impeccable suit, lowering himself onto these worn, red, cord-covered pews, that are a little stained. He's an enigma. But he's right about one thing – it is a great place to people-watch.

I am especially fascinated by the way parents behave around their children; I imagine what I would do in their position. I watch a young mother lose her temper, trying to fold her screaming toddler in half to get him into his pushchair; if it were me, I'd just let him walk, and everything would have to take as long as it took. It doesn't escape me that this is probably an easy thing for me to say, not being in that position, but I do believe I'd make a concerted effort to be patient, and to teach rather than bully. It's jealousy – I know it is – but I look at all these teenagers mooching around, smoking while they push their prams, and I think, 'Why have they been given the chance, and not me?' They're still children – I actually have something to teach, and I'm not bitter that my freedom has been taken away – I wouldn't ask a friend to babysit in order for me to go out and get smashed at the weekend – I'm way beyond all that. I'd appreciate my gift. I'd treasure, and nurture him or her … and it's become such a habitual train of thought, that I go round in circles in my head, until I remember: there is no reason why *I* can't have a child – it's not me who is the problem.

I am so deeply lost in thought, that Sasha startles me when he places a hand on my shoulder and greets me. This makes him chuckle, but before I have chance to worry about whether I should shake his hand, hug him, or kiss him on both cheeks, he asks me what I'd like to drink.

My cappuccino arrives, topped with a clump of chocolate sprinkles. Sasha laughs when I raise my eyebrows in displeasure, and I smile, feeling a little embarrassed. As I'd imagined, Sasha takes his coffee black, but it does surprise me when he adds three spoonfuls of sugar. White sugar. Of course, he notices this, and comments, "It's amusing, isn't it – all the little judgements we unconsciously make about people." He raises his eyes from the metal sugar bowl, to my face, and says simply, "Julia, honestly, there's no need to be embarrassed! Everyone does it, all the time – it's an innate way of making sense of the world. But haven't you ever heard the phrase 'Don't judge a book by its cover'?" He tilts his head to the side, in a gesture that's reminiscent of Erazmus, but he is smiling, widely.

Initially I return his smile, but then my thoughts turn to Erazmus. I didn't know he'd been having an affair … an affair with a woman half his age … a patient … a vulnerable woman … he's abused his position … he's impregnated her. And then it hits me. The girl says Erazmus is the father of the baby she's carrying. How can he be? I've never conceived; and now I have the test results, I know there's nothing wrong with me, which means there has to be something wrong with Erazmus. And *that* means the girl is lying!

Momentarily, I am filled with joy, but it dissipates when I realise that not being the father of the girl's baby doesn't detract from the fact that there is no smoke without fire, and whatever the truth is, Erazmus has kept things hidden from me, *and* walked out on me.

"If only he'd *talked* to me!" The sentence springs from my lips, and I'm suddenly painfully aware of the fact that I've been staring at Sasha. He smiles apologetically and says that he hadn't meant to upset me. He gestures to the waitress to bring us more coffee, and after glancing at his watch, he listens while I unburden myself, answering my questions as they come up.

"Anyway, what about you, Sasha?" I ask, finally, partly because I want to stop my own train of thoughts, partly out of politeness, and partly because I'm genuinely interested. Sasha Grosvenor fascinates me. If I'm honest with myself, he's always fascinated me. Maybe Erazmus and I aren't so different after all. I allow anger and affront to rise in me again, because it gives me permission to enjoy the tingling sensation I have, sitting here, being with this man.

Sasha is extremely intelligent and diligent, but simultaneously, if I was a stranger, passing him in the street, I'd describe him as an oddball. I nod at the pile of papers he'd placed on the end of the table earlier. "Are you working on a book, or is this preparation for your working day?"

Sasha smiles a tight smile. Erazmus always looks over his glasses when he's communicating on a personal level; Sasha looks straight through his, and rarely blinks. The effect is intense. I wonder how bad his sight is. "It's neither, actually," he replies. "This is research for a personal project."

"Oh?" I pause, hinting at him to elaborate. He doesn't.

His gaze consumes me, and I blush. He gives a warm smile, and his eyes flash. "Do you have any personal projects, Julia?"

And that's how it begins.

Later, walking back through the grey streets to my car, trying to control the butterflies in my stomach, the sentence about Erazmus that had spilled from my lips pops into my head again – 'If only he'd talked to me'.

Erazmus *does* talk to me, maybe not always with words, but he does tell me. Every night he spends in the spare room, he tells me. He tells me without telling me, and he's been telling me for years. But I've been telling him for years, too. It makes me laugh to think that two intelligent people have muddled along for so long, because they don't know what to do, hoping that time will heal. Is that what marriage is? Or is that what love is? Or is it a cop-out? Anger is easy. Anger is so easy, and I let it mix deliciously with the butterflies, and when I start up my car, I realise I haven't felt so alive in years.

Erazmus

"Faye ... please. I am literally begging you. I hate to put you in a difficult position ... surely that tells you how important this is to me."

I've been extremely fortunate. As I exited the roundabout and turned into the hospital car park, I noticed Faye Farefield's burgundy Astra pulling out of the staff parking section. I blocked the junction, so as she reached it, she had no choice but to acknowledge me. I gesticulated to her to follow me to the far end of the car park. Her expression was grave, and she slowly shook her head in exasperation at herself; then she acquiesced.

"Erazmus. We've worked together for many, many years, but you of all people should understand that this would mean putting my career in jeopardy, and ...".

"I do, but ...".

"This involves an esteemed colleague, and a patient of mine. I honestly didn't believe the allegations to begin with, but clearly they're true. Erazmus, what were you – what are you thinking?!"

I glance around again, to check that we haven't been seen, then put my hands in my hair, spin around, and kick my driver's side wheel. I stare Faye right in the face.

"I think I love her, Faye. I need to put things right."

Faye shakes her head in disbelief, but I keep my expression level, and eventually she stares seriously at me.

I know she isn't happy – either with me, or the situation – but something in me makes her take the note from my hand. I'm suddenly aware that I know very little of her, on a non-professional level. I don't even know if she has any children, or a marriage. As soon as this thought passes through my mind, I glance down at her left hand, but she snatches the paper I'm holding, and spins off in the direction of the doctor's surgery, leaving her car ticketless in a public space. I fumble in my trouser pocket for some change, and realise I left my last pound coin with the librarian. I have enough, though, and brave the walk to the ticket machine. Cursing the fact that the maximum stay was two hours, I buy Faye a ticket, wipe the droplets from a patch of her windscreen, and place the ticket under her driver's side wiper. I don't think anyone has seen me.

On the drive back to Swansburne, my thoughts are about Julia. The days have slipped by almost imperceptibly, and she'll be worrying about me, I know she will. Additionally, I have, to all intents and purposes, disappeared off the face of the earth; Julia, however, is at home with the telephone, the answerphone, and the letterbox. Remembering that my pager is in the glove compartment of my car, I am compelled to pull over and check it. No messages. I turn around in the car park of a pub called the Heron in a nearby village, retrace my route, and drive to the school where Julia works. The car park there only has spaces for the staff's cars, so I pull in at the kerb, halfway up Marina Way, and walk the short distance to the school. When I arrive at the red brick building near the canal, I'm not wholly surprised that Julia's car isn't there; however, I do feel a little disappointed in her. I thought she had more backbone than that.

I lean on the old wooden gate and gaze down into the playground, where the children have just been called in from their morning break. Some of them run in as soon as Mrs Brookes has rung the bell; some dawdle, kicking their ball between them as they go; one little girl walks in holding Mrs Brookes' hand. I pity Julia in that moment, seeing other people's children grow and change; however, I feel no yearning to be a father. Ending our marriage is the right thing to do, but I can't speak to someone who isn't here.

As I turn away to return to my car, Julia's friend, Shirley, runs out of the building calling to me. My heart sinks.

"Erazmus! Hi! Is Julia okay? What's going on?"

"Hello, Shirley. Yes, Julia's all right – she's just … feeling unwell How are you?"

"Oh, thank goodness! But then, what are you doing here? I thought you'd come to bring in her death certificate, or something!"

I give a small laugh, shaking my head, while I scan my mind for a plausible answer. "Nothing like that, thankfully, Shirley. I've had an – intense – morning at work and need some fresh air, so I'm going for a short walk along the canal to clear my head. I parked just down the road, so was literally just passing by." I smile.

"Well, the air's certainly fresh enough!" Shirley visibly relaxes. "Tell Julia to get well soon, and to give me a ring! And watch you don't get blown into the water – one of our pupils did, on the way home yesterday – luckily a man was jogging by at the time and managed to pull her out!"

I smile again. Shirley is prone to exaggeration, so the chances of her account being correct are slim. "That was fortunate," I comment, trying to hide my contempt for this woman. "But I'm sure I'll be fine. It was nice to see you, Shirley, and I'll pass your message on to Julia. Have a good day."

"Thanks, and the same to you. Actually, it's nice to know that Julia's human, and can actually get ill, like the rest of us! By the way, my ex-husband used to have a coat like that! See you!"

As I turn away from the school gate for the second time, I curse my brain. It's extremely cold, and I now have to go for a walk. But I'm glad that Shirley hadn't noted that I was not in my usual work attire.

Stuffing my hands into what might well have been Shirley's ex-husband's coat, I grit my teeth and cross the road to the gate that leads onto the canal. Initially I turn left, but the icy blast of the wind in my face is too much to bear, so I turn and stride in the other direction, hoping that the wind drops before I have to head back.

The canal is one of this town's most popular tourist attractions. Shire horses still pull the ornate barge. Julia and I once walked the length of it for a charity event; it was a pleasant, if easy, walk – quiet, scenic, and there's a nice pub that backs onto it at Sampford Peverell. Today, though, it's not so much fun; the biting wind, albeit from behind me, the darker-than-slate-grey sky, mirrored by the stagnant water, the new leaves clinging onto their branches for dear life – even the waterfowl are hiding. This particular stretch of the waterway is bordered by a council estate on one side, and the bungalows of the wealthy retirees on the other. Julia said that we'll 'downsize' to one of them, one day; one of the ones with the decking at the bottom of the sloping garden, with a place to dock a rowing boat. I let the comment go – everyone on the towpath could see not just the whole length of the gardens, but through the inevitable patio doors and into the living rooms, too. Maybe that's the point.

I intended to turn back when I came to the green bridge, near Wilcombe School, but as I approach, something makes me sit down on one of the memorial benches and observe for a moment, instead. There's a young man standing in the middle of the bridge, staring into the water. I guess he's an adolescent, but he might be older – it's hard to tell, these days. He has curly, blond hair, but I can't see his face because his forehead is resting – is pressed hard – on the side of the bridge, and he's turning his head from side to side. He's openly sobbing. I have seen people in all kinds of states during my career, but this young man is the epitome of grief. His hands are stretched out in front of his head, over the side of the bridge, and they are clasping something blue. I have the uncharacteristic urge to rush along the bridge and comfort him, but common sense prevails, and I sit on the memorial bench trying not to look like I'm watching him. I wonder for a moment if he's going to jump, but the bridge is so low, and the water so shallow, that unless he plunges headfirst and gets stuck in the canal's fetid bed, there's no way he could end his life – even if he can't swim, he'll be able to stand up and walk out, unless he simply submerges himself and inhales. Seeing him so desperate, chilled to the bone as I am, I feel somehow responsible for his safety, so determine to stay as

103

long as he does. Although I'm partly shielded from the wind by some thick brambles and the trunk of an oak tree, I pull up the hood of my new parka, thrust my hands as deep as they'll go into my pockets, and even pull them up into the sleeves of my jacket. I'm shivering. The young man has no coat – he's wearing a grey and black flecked jumper, jeans and trainers – but the cold is clearly not even registering for him.

Eventually, the blond man looks up into the compassionless sky. His face is pale but blotchy, his mouth slightly open. He drops his gaze to whatever he's clutching in his still-outstretched hands, is motionless for a second, and then let's the blue object drop. He turns in my direction, meets my eyes for a beat, then scurries off the bridge and into the council estate.

I stand and rush to the water's edge. The object he's dropped is a baby's soft toy – a forget-me-not blue octopus, with beady eyes and a smiling mouth. I scan the bushes for a long branch with which to retrieve it, but the toy is too far out. I watch its eyes as it slowly sinks beneath the stagnant surface of the grey water.

Lizzie

They tell me that my family are here to visit me, but I shake my head, refusing to see them. Dr Farefield is brought in – wearing beige, with that freaky cheetah broach as usual – in the hopes that, as my family doctor, she will have more sway over me; I do not look her in the eyes. She asks whether I would like to see Dom, and the question tears that animal sound from me again.

When I wake up, Dr Farefield is still here, but in different clothes. She looks – *dodgy* – her eyes are too bright and wet. She catches me looking at her before I can close my eyes again; she rests her hand on my shoulder, and brings her face in close.

"Lizzie. Would it help you to have contact with Erazmus?"

I catch myself nodding violently, my vision blurred by hot, fat tears. I turn my head quickly from side to side, and I feel the sound rising in me, but Dr Farefield places both her hands firmly onto my shoulders. The warmth of her hands spreads into me, and I realise that I am otherwise very cold.

"Lizzie. It's okay. He wants to see you – not in a bad way!" she adds, as I take a breath and open my mouth. "I shouldn't be doing this, so do not breathe a word of it, but he's written you a note – I can show it to you so that you can read it, but you won't be able to keep it. Would you like to read it?"

I do not move my body, but I stare into her jewel-like eyes, and nod, once.

Dr Farefield glances around her, then pulls a folded slip of paper from the pocket of her dress. For an instant, she expects me to take it from her, but shakes her head at herself when she remembers my bandaged hands. I am still

105

horizontal, so she unfolds it and holds it open above me. I don't think she has read it – she has integrity – and I suppose that she can't tell anyone what she doesn't know.

There's not much to read – I pretty much instantly nod, to indicate that I have read it, and that she should put it away. I turn my face to the wall. He says that he cares 'deeply' for me; that he will put things right. He thanks me for his 'fake plastic' cactus. I stare at the wall until I hear Dr Farefield sigh, then listen to the clip-clop of her footsteps until they fade away.

Julia

The following day, Sasha and I leave the coffee shop together. I know my face is flushed, and I try my hardest to push the excited teenager in me down and make this appear like a business meeting; not that anyone I know sees us, or anyone else is even remotely interested in us, but I am haunted by my emotional betrayal of Erazmus, and I'm sure that everyone we pass can feel the guilt radiating off me. Then I catch myself – Erazmus has done this, not me. He betrayed me first. I wince at the childishness of that thought, but harden myself – I have to do something for me now. As Erazmus had said, I'm not getting any younger.

Sasha and I have both parked in the market car park, and the weather is so awful neither of us want to be out in it any longer than entirely necessary. We cross the road, walk under the coach house – I don't know whether it's used for offices for the shops on either side, or if it's someone's grotty flat – and over to the main parking places by the pannier market. I stop as we arrive at my car, but Sasha puts a firm hand on my elbow, and guides me on and through the gap in the ancient-looking stone wall that runs along the back of the parking area. Electricity buzzes through me. On the other side of the wall is a narrow path and a ditch that I presume used to carry a stream. The opposite wall has been topped with large shards of glass, to deter people from climbing it and entering the private properties beyond. There's a junk shop that advertises itself as an antiques emporium, but it's closed. As soon as we step under the arch, Sasha roughly pushes me to the left, and up against the wall. He kisses me deep and hard, and quickly. Then he smiles and says, "Until we meet again." And then he's gone.

Sitting behind the wheel of my car, I take a moment to recover myself with some deep breaths before reversing out of my space and driving home. Once inside, I go straight up to the bathroom, shower again, and change my clothes. I rub lots of moisturiser into my cheeks and chin, and put Vaseline on my lips – Sasha's face, though clean-shaven, had been rough, and the skin around my mouth is reddened. I'll let it all soak in for a while, before reapplying my make-up.

Downstairs in the kitchen, I put the kettle on to boil, and put four scoops of coffee into the cafetiere. I stand there, tapping my fingers on the worktop, before realising that I'm literally watching a kettle boil, so I sit at our – the – beautiful kitchen table, and pick up the Gazette. I flick through it, absently, before realising that I haven't bought a newspaper. That's when I notice the flowers and the envelope.

So Erazmus has been back. I consider dumping the flowers – white roses and lilies – partly because giving flowers in this situation is such a clichéd and empty gesture, and partly because I don't know what he's trying to say, if indeed he's trying to say anything. I put the roses in a vase instead. They're pretty, and I don't want them to have been picked just to go in a bin, but lilies are poisonous to cats – surely Erazmus knows that?

I sit back down, with my strong, steaming coffee, and open the envelope. Fly appears from nowhere, jumps onto my lap and starts spuddling. His claws catch in my tights – another pair I'll have to throw away. Erazmus is a sticker-down of envelopes, whereas, unless they're going in a post box, I always just fold the flap in. I read the note, then scrunch it up in my fist and throw it as far as I can. It's been handwritten – or, rather, scrawled – on a piece of paper that's obviously been torn from one of his notebooks, and simply states that he'd hoped to see me, that there was something important that he needed to tell me, and that he would be away for another week. I was not to worry about him, and he hoped I would be feeling better soon.

Adrenalin and guilt immediately rush through me – Erazmus knows that I haven't been to work – but I push the

108

uncomfortable feelings down. He can think what he likes; he's in the wrong here, not me, and his scrappy note hasn't given any kind of apology or explanation whatsoever. I run a finger over my lips, remembering Sasha's kiss, and smile to myself. I love the irony of it: Erazmus has chosen to be 'away' for a week, which clears the way for me to spend time with Sasha.

As I drive out of the town and up into the steep hills that cradle it, I fervently hope that I won't get lost, or meet another car and have to reverse on these narrow country lanes, but Sasha's instructions are clear – "Keep going in as straight a line as you can, until you see my house sign on the left." I'm there within fifteen minutes.

'Nether Cullen' fits my preconception of Sasha's home perfectly. When I turn off the lane, I start bumping along his half-mile-long drive in second gear and soon have to change into first. Wild brambles border the makeshift concrete road which slopes down at quite a gradient. There are no streetlights for miles around here, and it seems as if I'm falling down the yellow tunnel made by my headlights. Eventually, I see lights high up and on my right, and another sign for Nether Cullen. I have to rev hard to get up to the double garage, outside which Sasha's dark green Jaguar is parked.

I'm trembling when I step out of my car. Sasha's house is the only inhabited one in a mews of newly converted barns. The communal area is a hexagonal lawn with a tall rowan tree at its centre. There's a lit wrought iron Victorian lamppost outside a heavy oak front door, so I make my way towards it and bang on the door with the lion head knocker. The ornate brass is painfully cold to touch, and I blow on my hands and tuck them under my arms as I wait for the click of Sasha's footsteps to increase in volume and then halt. He opens the door with a wide smile.

"Welcome," he announces. "Enter freely and of your own free will!" He says the last bit with a sideways smile, and I feel like I've missed a joke, so I laugh and pretend I haven't.

He steps aside theatrically, and gestures with a sweeping arm for me to step inside.

The hall is long and narrow, and hung with dark paintings in gilt frames which shine in the glow of the ceiling lights. It's painted a deep red, and the floorboards are bare, almost ebony, and highly polished. Sasha leads me to another heavy door, that has elaborate iron hinges, and opens it onto a vast yet warm, and comfortable country kitchen. There's a well-used Aga, at the foot of which a thin black cat sleeps on a tartan rug. I think of Fly – he would love this! I follow Sasha through the kitchen and round to the right, and we step up into his lounge. A wood-burner emits so much warmth that I remove my cardigan.

Sasha motions me to join him sitting on a low, soft leather sofa. It has wide seats, and tartan blankets hang over its back; I long to snuggle under one and watch the flames from the wood-burner flicker. On an even lower oak coffee table stands an open bottle of red wine, the type of which I don't recognise, two crystal glasses, some After Eight mints and a Newton's cradle.

Sasha pours us both a glass, and turns to face me, his arm slung casually along the back of the sofa. I sip my wine and smile, glancing around the room at the tightly packed bookshelves, the wooden beams, the plush carpet. With the exception of a porcelain bay horse and the Newton's cradle, there are no ornaments or photographs – for all its cosiness, this is undoubtedly a single man's home.

I let my eyes meet his, and the rush I feel through my body is so intense, I gasp. Sasha's smile widens. He removes his glasses, placing them on the coffee table, slides across the sofa until our legs are touching, leans forward, and kisses me again.

The fire in the wood-burner has all but died out when I wake, but the room is still warm. Sasha is still asleep. We lie, tangled up in each other's limbs, on the rug, and Sasha must have covered us with the blanket from the back of the sofa while I slept. I have no idea what the time is, but it's still dark outside, and for the first time in my entire life, I don't care.

Sasha had been so different to Erazmus. With my husband, sex feels like something that has to be done to fulfil an innate need – like eating, or going to the toilet – and once he's got it out of his system, he's somehow okay again; he locks the regretful animal in him back into its box in his head, and goes back to being an intelligent human getting on with the important things in his life – the things *he* considers to be important in his life.

I should be the most important thing in his life; my needs should be the most important thing in his life. I can't understand it – he'd loved me fiercely at one time. When had that died? And why? And if he's such an intelligent human being, why hasn't he fixed this?

Sasha must have felt me tense, because he stirs; without opening his eyes, and without words, he makes love to me again. And the next time I become aware of my surroundings, particles are dancing in a ray of sunshine that's penetrated a gap in the curtains.

Sasha isn't beside me on the floor any more. I sit up and cover myself with the blanket. The fire is dead now, and there's a chill in the room. Looking around, I notice that last night's debris has been removed, and there's a cafetiere of steaming coffee on the low table, next to a white cup and saucer with matching milk jug and sugar bowl. The sugar is cubed – white on one side, demerara on the other – and there are tongs on the side. I smile at first, but then the guilt rushes in: I don't take sugar – Sasha and I do not know each other well – I have just committed adultery. I try to justify my actions by reminding myself that Erazmus did it first, but I can't fool myself – I can't undo what I've done.

Naked under the blanket, I kneel up and pour myself a coffee, but it only exacerbates the foul taste in my mouth. The house is silent, and presuming Sasha has left for work, I stand, gather up my clothes and search for the bathroom. I step down from the lounge into the cavernous dining room. The ceiling is extremely high, and the people who had converted the barn had left the beautiful original oak beams.

A literally sparkling chandelier hangs from a long chain over an oak dining table, and the walls are basically bookcases. I peer at some of the titles – most of them are medical tomes, but squashed in between two thick hardbacks is a small, battered paperback – *The Horse Whisperer* by Nicholas Evans. My gut screams at me to take the book out and flip through it, but I need to shower and collect myself first. I find the stairs behind a wooden door, and ascend, my feet luxuriating in the plush carpet.

At the top of the straight stairs is a square landing, with two bedrooms and a bathroom off each of the three remaining sides. I'm tempted to look in the bedrooms, but the urge to get clean curbs my curiosity, so I push the wooden door open, and step into a forest-green tiled bathroom. It's immaculate – there isn't even a droplet of water on the side of the sink. I wonder how much time Sasha spends cleaning – does he have a cleaner, or does he have OCD? And what time is it? The shower floor is dry, but my coffee had been hot. Letting the tartan blanket drop to the floor, I reach into the shower cubicle, pull the gold lever, and wait for the torrent of water to begin to steam.

I step in before I realise there are no toiletries in the cubicle. I glance round for a shelf, or for a replica of the cluster of bottles that gather dust and soap scum around the sink in my own home. I notice a cupboard set into an ornamental arch in the opposite corner of the room. As the towel that should be hanging over the radiator is absent too, I lean out, grab the blanket, and dry myself as best I can, so that I won't drip water on the wooden floor. I pick a fluffy white towel from one of the neatly stacked piles in the cupboard, hoping that Sasha won't mind, and am relieved to find some Molton Brown shower gel and shampoo. Both are unopened. Sasha's house – I'm having trouble thinking of it as his home – is so like a hotel, that I wonder if he lives here at all. But then he is eccentric and successful, and that's attractive; I find myself mirroring the caresses of his hands as I wash my body.

I gasp when I see him standing there, a foot away from the

shower cubicle, watching me, smiling. His smile widens at my horror, and he removes his glasses, jacket and shoes, saying, "Please, Julia, don't be embarrassed." He opens the door, and steps inside, his shirt instantly soaked to the skin. He takes my startled face in his hands and kisses me deeply. "I went out to get the papers," he says, pouring a thick line of shower gel around my shoulders and across my throat, and then he begins to wash me.

I call Mark at the school on Friday, as I'd promised, and inform him that although my tests results have come back clear, I'm experiencing an exceptionally stressful time in my personal life, and that I'll need another week off, asking that he take the time off my annual leave as I don't have a diagnosis, and feel terribly guilty about being unable to work. His tone of voice conveys his concern; he says that I shouldn't underestimate the effects of stress, that I should go back to the doctor's and get a certificate, and that as I'm sick, I will receive sick pay.

I spend Friday night with Sasha, but drive home in the morning to see to Fly and sort things out. I need to clear my head, think about Erazmus' return, and make solid plans for my future. Our marriage is over – that truth has finally hit me – there is no going back from any of this. I need to find a divorce lawyer, put the house on the market, find a temporary place to live. Part of me is desperate to ask Sasha if I can stay with him, but I don't want to put pressure on what is an extremely enjoyable budding relationship. Also, there's Fly to think about. I return to Sasha's house on Saturday evening, but have to tear myself away from him early on Sunday morning, when he receives a call from The Meadows, asking him to come in for an urgent meeting.

I can't wait to meet Sasha at the Mad Hatters on Tuesday morning. My body tingles all over, and I feel a great rush of heat when I see him sitting at what I now consider to be 'our' table, completely absorbed in whatever it is that he's writing. I sit down opposite him because there are files and paper piled up on either side of him. He looks up, brushes my arm with his fingertips, watches the heat rush through me again, and then, looking me straight in the eyes, he says, "Your husband has been reinstated."

Time stands still. My mouth is dry and, realising it's open, I close it. "Wh … What?"

"Elizabeth retracted her statement. The following day, she attempted to climb the fence of the secure hospital at which she was a voluntary patient. Consequentially, she has been moved, and is no longer hospitalised voluntarily. Your husband is keen for things to 'get back to normal' as soon as possible, and will resume his post on Monday," the twitch through Sasha's face is almost imperceptible, "which means that I return to my lowly status as his understudy." He gives a hollow laugh. "In addition to this, so I am informed, he has completed his eagerly anticipated book, and it is being edited as we speak!" Sasha smiles, but his eyes are black. I have no idea how to respond.

He stares at me, the hollow smile frozen on his face, and waits; clearly a technique he practises with his patients.

"But that doesn't mean you and I have to … does it?" And there it is – my relationship with Sasha has become the priority in my life. He tilts his head to the side, and smiles, running his leg as far up mine as he can, under the table. The heat pulses through me again.

"No," he says, his eyes triumphant. "No, it doesn't."

Erazmus

The isolation, the sea air, and the anonymity of my room in the bed and breakfast are just what my mind and spirit have been crying out for. I write and write, the days and nights blur, and on the Friday before my fortnight is up, I have my first draft. I'm jubilant.

And then, finally, I get paged. Although there had been no messages on it when I'd checked the day I tried to see Julia, I decided I ought to keep it charged – partly in the hopes that Faye Farefield will give me an update on Lizzie – and I put it in my trouser pocket, as is my habit. Then, at just after six on Friday evening, it beeps.

There's a message from The Meadows. Lizzie has retracted her statement, and I should contact the department immediately. I don't. I take another freezing walk along the sea wall, letting the violent waves splash me as they crash up against it, while I decide which course of action to take.

I walk to Cardinal's Cove again, listening to the gulls shriek as they shoot across the dark, tempestuous sky. A man walking his dog briskly back towards the town warns me in his broad accent that I ought to go home too, before I get into trouble. I smile and thank him, but I rest my shins up against the low, white wall, and nod acknowledgement at the battered red rock on which sea birds rest, that holds its own against the ocean, only about fifty yards from the shore. Then I turn my gaze back inland, and up to the tree that stands precariously close to the cliff edge. I've walked this way many times over the last fortnight and have become fascinated by this tree. I wonder if I climb the winding path to the top, locate the tree and give it a shove, whether it will finally meet the waves; if it will gladly meet the waves.

A sudden splatter of brine on my back jerks me out of my

reverie, and I realise that the tide has come so far in that the water has entirely covered the sand in the cove and is hitting the rusty cliffs; I finally heed the stranger's warning, and retrace my steps. When I reach the little harbour, Boat Cove, I know that it would be madness to attempt to walk back along the sea wall – an InterCity 125 rockets through, and I watch, by the glow from the streetlights that are now on, and the train's headlights, an enormous wave come over the wall and smash against the carriages before the train disappears into the tunnel. I run to the iron bridge, my footsteps clanging on the metal, and over it, to the relative safety of Marine Parade. I walk quickly, scanning the streets for a phone box, and when I find one, I dial the number for The Meadows, telling them shortly that I will be back at work on Monday, and that I expect a sincere apology. Then I hang up, and walk the length of the stream in the gathering gloom.

I'm not surprised to feel sad, packing my few clothes, and all my papers and notebooks into the boot of my car. I have the nagging feeling that I'm waving goodbye to my freedom. A train rushes past me and stops at the station, and I have an urge to run the short distance to it and jump on board with no thought to its destination; but I stand with my car door open in the Baltic wind and watch it disappear, heading out of the West Country, gathering speed. I slide in behind the steering wheel, slam the door, and put the car into reverse, catching sight of the B & B in the corner of my rear-view mirror. I almost expect Grace to be standing on the step, waving me off, and am disappointed that she's not.

Turning left and following the one-way system, I glance in my mirror until I can no longer see the ocean. The primary-coloured lights over the stream are bright against the brooding clouds, and I can hear the tinny music from the big arcade on my right. I have always hated that noise, so I switch on the car stereo. Radiohead. This time, I let the album play. I want to put my foot down, but it's impossible to do safely on the winding A roads, so when I reach Exeter, I followed the signs for the M5, and blast up the motorway back to Eskwich.

I drive straight home, releasing the inevitable tension in my shoulders and jaw whenever I become aware of it. Julia's car is not on the drive when I reach our house. I reverse into my usual space and sit in the car with the engine off for a few minutes while I compose myself. I look at the neat houses and gardens, smile at our neighbours as they walk by with their golden retriever. With my arms full of my papers, I awkwardly unlock the front door, and shove it open with my shoulder. The house is clearly unoccupied. After placing my papers on the desk in the office Julia and I share, I have a long, hot shower, change my clothes, and make a cafetiere of coffee. While it brews, I head on autopilot to put my dirty clothes in the laundry basket. I'm surprised to find it full – Julia is verging on obsessed with the washing machine, and even though there are only two of us in the household, she still manages to do a load every other day.

There are no newspapers on the kitchen table, and I hadn't thought to buy one, so I sit at the table with my coffee and let the thoughts pass through my mind. Something strikes me, so I go back upstairs and look inside the laundry basket again. The clothes which fill it are not ones that Julia wears to work. They are what she calls her 'nice' clothes – the garments she saves for nights out with Shirley, or the rare occasions we attend dinner parties. Perhaps she's taken some time off, and has been away – after all, I have. Once I've finished my coffee, I pour myself another and return to the office. Speculation isn't productive.

The bang of the wind slamming the front door closed interrupts my thoughts.

"Erazmus?" I take a deep breath, put my papers in order, and listen to Julia rummaging in her handbag, taking off her coat, and making the sounds of complaint people seem unable not to utter when they come in out of bad weather. When it becomes apparent that she isn't going to come upstairs, I pad down. She's still in the hall, folding a slip of paper.

"Hello, Julia." She spins round in surprise, fumbling with

the paper, which falls to the floor. Instinctively, I track its descent to the carpet – it's a reminder for a doctor's appointment. Julia gasps, snatches it up, and stuffs it into her bag. She's very pale, but her cheeks are flushed scarlet.

"Are you okay?" I ask, nodding to the bag which now holds the appointment details.

"Yes, yes – it's just for a quick check-up in a couple of weeks," she gabbles. She gives a quick smile, which leaves her face before she adds, "Erazmus, I don't know what to say. I heard that you've been reinstated. I'm sorry." Julia's eyes flick to the floor before she raises them to meet mine again, with a searching expression.

"I'm sorry, too," I say. Neither of us states what we are sorry for, and we stand awkwardly in the hall for a few seconds, before I fill the silence with, "Do you think we can work through this, Julia?"

"Yes, of course we can!" Julia's face breaks into a warm smile, and she steps towards me, so I open my arms and hold her. She answered too quickly.

Julia

I honestly do not know how to feel, because I feel so much, and whatever perspective I choose, I feel something different. The emotion that overrides all the others, though, is fear. I will lose something, I know I will.

The day Erazmus came home was the day I kind of subconsciously knew I was pregnant. I don't know how I knew, and if I'd taken a test it would have been too early for it to show up, but I knew. And suddenly Erazmus wants us to try again. I said that I would, even though I have a meeting with my solicitor about filing for divorce, and am viewing a flat later in the week.

I knew I would conceive with Sasha. I made this happen. I haven't told him, because I am so uncertain how he will react. But it's all really early days, yet. I have time enough to set myself up as an independent woman, and make things secure for my child.

I am sitting in my car in the hospital car park, waiting for ten minutes to pass – I like to be five minutes early for appointments, but no more than that. I consider being too early as rude, if not more rude than being late.

When I enter the surgery, the warmth of the waiting room immediately relaxes me. The carpet and walls are soft shades of blue, the furniture an oak-coloured wood. I sit in a straight-backed chair as far away from other patients as I can, right next to the patio doors, which is nice, because I can watch the traffic passing and the trees being buffeted by the wind, instead of staring at the floor trying not to make eye contact with anyone. It also means I am near the children's area. I watch a young mum sitting with her baby between her outstretched legs on the colourful rug, reading a well-thumbed copy of *Where the Wild Things Are*. The child is mesmerised by the story, and doesn't notice that his mother keeps moving slightly away from him, to see if he can support himself sitting up. After a time, he manages it, just for a few seconds before falling back onto his mum's tummy. She finds this miraculous, and covers his blond head in kisses. My eyes begin to well up, and I place both hands gently over my abdomen. If I can have just one moment like that in my life, anything else that happens will be collateral damage.

For people like me – those with family who work in the NHS, especially in a small town – seeking healthcare can be awkward. I am fully aware that every healthcare professional has taken an oath of confidentiality, but there's always a part of me that thinks that they're only human, and everyone lets off steam somehow. I wonder about the stories Dr Farefield's husband must have heard over the years, and the raised eyebrows and smirks in the surgery staff room at lunchtime; I wonder about the things Erazmus and Faye share, to which I am not party. However, I don't feel like I can go to anyone but my family doctor with my pregnancy – I'd trust Faye with my life. I just have to trust her with my secret.

Dr Farefield likes to come out of her consultation room and ask for her patients by name, and when she spots me in the waiting room, she smiles widely.

On hearing my news, Faye's smile almost splits her face in two. She laughs, and comments that 'miracles do happen', how 'things that are meant to be, will be', how people should 'never give up hope', and that she'll congratulate Erazmus when she sees him in the morning. I break down at that, and whisper that Erazmus doesn't know, and ask if she could not mention the pregnancy to him until I've had more time to think about it. The joy drains from her face at that, and she apologises profusely; then I apologise for putting her in an awkward position, and she apologises for being unprofessional and over-familiar, and then she gives me the spiel, and we plan a course of action. Although Faye states that pregnancy tests today are so reliable, they render blood tests unnecessary, I beg her to take a vial to check that there's nothing wrong with me or the foetus, and she does; but she does it with shaking hands, and I know I'll be bruised by the morning. I don't tell her that the baby is not Erazmus', but I know she's seen the truth in my eyes.

Sasha

The gleaming silver balls of my Newton's cradle clack together with purifying violence. I stare at them while my mind clears, and pour a second strong black coffee from the pot.

I've disinfected the bathroom, and my effects have been returned to their proper positions. The laundry is clean and is in the tumble drier. The wood-burner has fresh wood, I have polished every surface, and all the windows are open. I have showered with tea tree shower gel to disinfect myself, and I have used a considerable amount of mouthwash. I had to get every trace of that woman – and by default, that man – off me. It is exhausting, but I will not stop. I will not stop until Erazmus Whittle is dead.

Julia

Whenever I think I am getting that perfect scene from a movie, that moment I crave, something always happens to take the shine off. Every diamond I think I have turns out to be diamante, and then I have to convince myself and everyone else that, no, it's definitely a diamond, and things are okay.

Passionate people have extremes, I know that. I *know* that. Why do I never expect it?!

Sasha walked out on me yesterday evening. He walked out and drove off and left me on my own, and I spent the whole night crying, until I cried myself to sleep, and now I'm out on his drive in the early morning, crying again, wishing for his car to appear. The only sounds are the cawing of a murder of crows, and the wind in the trees. I go back inside. Eventually, I hear tyres on the gravel, and I run outside. Sasha slams his car door shut, and lurches round to face me. I gasp at the state of him. He is grinning, and his features are puffy, his eyes tiny and red. His jacket, waistcoat and tie are off, and he's gripping them tightly in his left hand as if he fears he'll lose them forever; in his right hand, he clasps the neck of a bottle of wine. His shirt is open four buttons down, and I can see his pale chest. He staggers over to me and throws both arms around me without letting go of anything. I stand stock-still, and nausea floods over me. He stinks. He stinks of cigarettes, stale alcohol, sweat, grease, and something sickeningly sweet that I can't identify.

"I apologise for my actions," he slurs. "Although I must admit, your words shocked me somewhat. Why don't you come inside – we can share this!" he says, holding the bottle aloft, beaming.

"I can't, Sasha," I reply. "I'm pregnant."

"Oh, come now, Julia! It's very early days, and I do like you a lot. You're … open to things most women are not, and I like that. Have one little glass with me, and we'll … talk things over."

"Okay," I say, smiling because I have no other option. I am suddenly aware that my teeth are feeling fuzzy, and there is a stale taste in my mouth. "But I need to freshen up first."

"How convenient!" Sasha shouts. "So do I! We'll have a shower, like we did the other morning. That will be a wonderfully invigorating start to the day!" The hand that has slipped down to my waist to guide me into his house, slides down a little further. I feel a pulse in my groin. Sasha kicks the door shut behind us.

Afterwards, there's no preamble, and little warmth. "Are you really pregnant, Julia?" he asks. I nod. "And is the baby really mine?" I nod again. "And what do you intend to do about it?" he asks, polishing his glasses with the special fluid and cloth he keeps in his inside pocket. As he finishes his last question, he puts them on. I feel like I am looking into the beam of a laser.

"What do you mean, 'do about it'?" I counter, feeling the adrenalin start to pump.

"I mean, do you intend to abort the pregnancy, or are you thinking you'll be able to keep it?"

"Why wouldn't I be able to keep it? And, sorry, but 'it'? This is our son or daughter we're talking about!" I'm incredulous. I feel the familiar bitterness rising up in me – the bitterness that I've always felt, because nothing happens for me like it should. That sounds childish and naïve, but it's absolutely true. I've always tried to do the right thing for everyone else, and I have received nothing in return!

It is absolutely clear to me that Sasha does not want this baby, but in spite of myself, I hear the question escaping my lips: "What would you like me to do?"

The question seems to slow time; so much so that I begin to feel content and numb. There is an ecstatic feeling of freedom that knowing you are on the verge of your life falling apart brings. It's freefall. There is nothing you can do about what you know is going to happen – the agency, but also the responsibility, has been taken from you. The irony is hysterical. Things will change, as of now, now and forever. A new life will begin. You have another chance to get the right outcome for you. You will die, or you will be strong – there is no middle ground – I am free.

I look to Sasha again, and find his expression has changed. "Why, Julia, I want you to keep him or her, of course! I'm terribly sorry if you misunderstood me!"

I am numb. Again. Sasha embraces me so tenderly, I sob. "If we have a girl," he murmurs into my ear, "would you mind if we call her Amber?" And all of a sudden, I have my perfect moment. He kisses me, slowly and deeply, and I cry as if my heart would break.

Then, there is the warm silence where we just hold each other and start to drift into sleep. It is so blissful, and my mind is numb and happy.

I stay at his house for a couple of days. I have never felt so wholly loved, cared for and fulfilled in my entire life. Sasha goes to work, but when he comes home, he cooks the evening meal. When I wake in the morning, there is a freshly brewed decaffeinated coffee, and a glass of pure orange juice waiting for me. He cooks wholesome meals, and there is always spinach in the salad. He encourages me to walk in the countryside, and to listen to the classical music he adores. Apparently, it is good for the baby's development. He has an extensive library in the spare bedroom which, unlike the shelves in Erazmus' office, are not filled only with scientific and medical reference books. I can't believe I had gone through my entire life so far without reading *Moby Dick*. I can't believe I had never heard of Rachmaninoff. And life goes on, and he invites me to Erazmus' book launch. I bask in my new-found happiness.

Sasha

It would have been Amber's twenty-fifth birthday today. I buy her a larger bouquet of yellow roses than usual on her birthday, and as this year would have been her quarter-century, there are twenty-five flowers. I'll commend them, one at a time, to the ocean, as I always do, in the place where I scattered her ashes – off the end of the pier. This necessitates an expedition to Tamehaven, but I generally feel better about things after the long, fast drive. I book this day off as annual leave every year, but I wasn't going to tell Julia that – I needed her out of my house as soon as I possibly could. Her breath! I plug in an air freshener even though the windows are open. I'd have the place fumigated, but she has been – and will no doubt continue to be – coming here (no pun intended) for some considerable time.

When the coffee pot is empty, I stop the Newton's cradle and put it back in its place. I rinse the pot, turn off the lights, and leave the house. Starting the car, I make a mental note to take it through a car wash before I head down the M5. The isolation of my house suits me, the inevitable mud, not so much. I have reached Eskwich town centre before I realise I have been driving in silence, so I press the button for the CD player. Bach's Toccata and Fugue in D Minor blares from my speakers. Perfect. Amber used to call it his 'Dracula music', and I smile at the memory. She could have been a professional violinist. She could have been a professional jockey – she loved horses. She could have been anything, but Whittle saw her as a victim, and brainwashed her into viewing herself in the same way. So that's what she became – a victim of manic depression. She could have lived an exceptional life – instead, she walked into the sea on her

126

birthday, and let the water pour into her lungs.

I go under the motorway bridge at Cullompton at exactly seventy miles an hour, because I know the police are lurking somewhere, waiting to pounce. I drive the rest of the way at ninety and above, sticking in the outside lane. As I'm approaching Splatford Split, I'm sure I see Whittle's hearse pass me on the other side of the central reservation. It might not have been him, but the thought is enough to force my right foot even further to the floor.

I tear up Haldon Hill, through the forest, across the moor-like land, before dropping down into Tamehaven. I laugh at the sign bearing the legend 'The Gem of South Devon'. Amber was The Gem of South Devon; she was the gem of my world.

The biggest car park in Tamehaven is the one right on the shore, opposite the Ness. In the winter, it gets battered by the ocean. This is where I park every time I come here. Once, the violent surges tore up the tarmac, and the police cordoned the area off. They had to force me to move, first. I had parked my car so that I was looking out to sea – right in front of the metal barrier. I sat there for a long time, staring out at the waves as they crashed over my windscreen. Eventually, shells and small pebbles started raining down on the car, but I didn't move until the police knocked on my window.

Now, in that same space, I sit and watch the furious waves breaking over the seawall, while I listen to the end of Toccata and Fugue in D Minor again. When I close my eyes, I can still see the water. The roses are on the passenger seat; I carefully remove the paper the florist has wrapped them in, and lay them back down, one at a time. They are fresh, perfect. Amber would have adored them. I exit my car. The wind whips my hair so it stings my cheeks, and as I walk past the redundant lighthouse and along the promenade to the pier, I am forced to keep wiping the salty spray from my glasses.

There are few people about, and I'm relieved to find the place open. Tamehaven Pier is a horrible mix of loud, gaudy arcade games, and severe Victoriana; it is also the place where Amber and I had some of the best times of our childhood.

Erazmus

Time has passed, and time has – to the innocent onlooker – healed.

My colleagues and I smile at each other when we pass in the corridors, in the car park, in the supermarket. Julia and I sleep in the same bed, and there has been no more talk of children. I have righted the howling mistakes Grosvenor made in my short absence, including revoking Kayleigh-Amanda Tarr's section, which I can't bring myself to comment on, but which I will most certainly explore in my next published work. My book is finished and is due for release in a week, and I am hosting a launch party of sorts. However, people talk about 'gut feelings', and I have the feeling that there is nothing 'right' or 'normal' about any of this. The thing that grates most is that Sasha Grosvenor has been allowed to remain working at The Meadows as my understudy.

Honestly, the impudence of the man! How thick can his skin be?! I'm not sure what he can have said to sway the powers that be – maybe he hypnotised them with his laser-like eyes, or just bored them to tears with the incessant monotone justification of his actions, which he has the audacity to stand by – but they appear to have bought his spiel about needing the opportunity to learn 'in the field'. There's something about him that doesn't ring true.

After a glass of wine at dinner, I decide to mention it to Julia, and she comments that if I wasn't a psychiatrist, she'd joke about me being paranoid. This is a ridiculous thing to say in any circumstance, but the fact that she sounds so flippant and silly really annoys me. I drain my glass and knock the bottle as I reach for it, sloshing the deep red liquid over the side and onto the tablecloth in my frustration.

I glance up at my wife, who hasn't noticed; she's absentmindedly prodding a piece of rocket with her fork, a small smile playing about her face. Shallow, I think. We've been sleeping together since my return – again, everything fine and back to normal on the surface – and when she goes up early, I bring another bottle and two glasses up with me. The thought that maybe I was using alcohol as a crutch flashes across my mind, but I push it down and, somewhat clumsily, climb the stairs.

Julia is reclining on the pillows in a black negligee that I don't recall having seen before. I pause – a little taken aback – and she spreads her legs, tilts her head to one side and smiles. This is totally out of character for her, and it angers me that she's suddenly inviting me like this, as if she is the one in control. I have used the term 'a red mist descended' on many occasions during my personal and professional life, but until this moment, I've never had a true understanding of its meaning. Internally, I'm consumed by it. I want to crush her. So I play along, because that's what it is – a game. I return her smile, remove my clothes and take her.

It's primal, and it's a power thing. She's excited at my roughness to begin with, but I can't stand her enjoyment. I know she wants this, not just to cement the revival of our relationship – a kind of twisted consummation – but because she feels these animal urges and lets them rule her. I'd discovered the Rampant Rabbit she had stashed under the bed years ago, when I was searching for a pen I'd mislaid. I never mentioned it to her. I'd been repulsed by it. And by her need, her indulgence and her secrecy. But here, I'm fully aware that the overriding reason for her smile is that she sees our congress as a chance for a baby. She's like a broken record; a CD with a scratch on it. So as I notice her climax starting to build, I withdraw, flip her over onto her belly and fuck her in her anus. She screams, but for once I let the animal in me take over, and I don't stop until I'm done.

Afterwards, we lie there in silence. In the morning, Julia is gone.

Presuming Faye Farefield did in fact deliver my note, there has been no kind of response from Lizzie, who remains in hospital. This doesn't appear to bother anyone. It's like she's been forgotten; dismissed as a drain on society. I wonder how many years it will be until economics dictate that the 'weaker' among us are not worth keeping alive. With the human population growing exponentially, I don't think it will be long. The mentally ill will be like stray dogs in an American animal rescue centre, but instead of someone coming to adopt them, it will be a case of 'get better, or die'. Prisons will become death camps, and I can envision the return of the death penalty. I'd expound on all these fears in a third book, but there are simply not enough hours in the day. The irony of all this is not lost on me. Writing dystopian novels is socially acceptable – 'cool', even – but there are not enough of us writing about it as scientific fact. Attitudes *have* to change. Lizzie is a person who needs *help*, not sedation. This epiphany is the closest I have ever come to madness – I know this because I know that it is futile, ridiculous, distracting, and yet I am powerless to stop it, because I know it is true.

I am no stranger to the university campus – I have trained here, taught here, lectured here and researched here. The University of Exeter is located just outside the city centre – the city centre being the cathedral grounds, and main shopping area – on a series of steep hills. It is both surrounded by and peppered with ancient trees, predominantly pines, some of which are gnarly, with thick crusts of grey-black bark peeling away. This accentuates the atmosphere of classical learning – the history and knowledge amassed here are palpable because of it. It is inspiring, exciting; the hill climbs that the students undertake to get to their seminars become metaphors, and when you reach the peak, you have the world at your feet, the city, and miles and miles of green hills beyond.

My book launch will take place in the at 7.30 in the evening, and is to be held in the Princess Alice building which, fortunately for the guests, is one of the first university buildings that you reach as you ascend. There are car parks, of course, but I am expecting many to walk in from the city centre, or arrive in taxis, as the alcohol will be plentiful. My introduction, readings, and the inevitable discussion are to take place in Lecture Theatre 1, with refreshments and mingling in the reception area, and in what is usually the cafe/work hall, to follow. There will be champagne on arrival.

I decide to drive in, which necessitates phoning the university and reserving a parking space in advance, but it also ensures that I will be sober, for one thing, and that I can get away when I like, for another. There are bound to be questions about the absence of Julia. Many of our friends are aware that she has been ill, but I do not know how many of them know that we are in the process of divorce. I cannot deny that rumours of a divorce would shed doubt on the validity of Lizzie retracting her statement.

My conscience forced me to add a kind of epilogue to my book – I'd disguised Lizzie's identity, as I had all the case studies in my work – because I had to state that Lizzie's mental health had deteriorated and that she was in fact back in hospital. When I'd started writing it, it felt like I was conceding that the care with which she had been provided had been somewhat inadequate; as I got further on, I felt that the point I was actually trying to make was that one can never predict Life (with a capital L), and that it was paramount for the mental health of every one of us to acknowledge that, at any given moment, we can only perform to the best of our ability, and that sometimes, in spite of our efforts, there will be losses. The brain is frequently likened to a computer – a machine – but it cannot be 'fixed' in the same way that a machine can be. Nor can we add hard drives or transfer excess data to disks. And even electroshock therapy cannot turn brains off and on again to reboot them. This is the place where physics and philosophy collide. Or, rather, where science and spiritualism collide. But then, without conflict, there is no story, and without story there is no evolution.

Finding myself unable to stay in the house any longer, I gather my suit, my smart shoes and my notes, and place them carefully in the boot of my car. I put down some extra biscuits for Fly, knowing that he will consume the lot as soon as he realises they are there, and leave for the event with hours to spare. As tonight is my night, I take *OK Computer* out of my car's CD player and replace it with *Back in Black*. As I approach Exeter, I realise that tonight is about Lizzie and those like her, not me, and I swerve the car off the hilly road to the university, and find myself heading through Exeter, with the intention of driving down the coast road to Swansburne, and from there to Tamehaven. I switch AC/DC for Radiohead. I cross the roundabout at Matford Marsh, and my speedometer is just showing 60 mph, when I hear sirens from behind me. I yank my Mercedes off the road and onto the patch of concrete under the motorway bridge to allow the ambulance to pass, and when I am back on the A379 again, I do not get far before I reach the point where the police are closing the road because of a crash. As there is nothing coming the other way, and there is nothing I can do, I have a word with the nearest officer, and make a U-turn. I will have to take the motorway, instead.

The drive to Tamehaven via the M5 is a metaphor for life. After the motorway becomes the A380 at the Bodmin turnoff, there's the curving descent to Splatford Split where the dual carriageway becomes a four-lane free-for-all, where everyone gets confused at 70 mph-plus, puts their foot down harder when the imposing climb that is Haldon Hill appears before them, and some then swerve at the last minute to get onto the Plymouth road from the inside lane to Tamehaven, or vice versa. There have been so many RTAs there, it doesn't bear thinking about. Which is ironic. The Devon Expressway veers off to the right, while the Tamehaven road goes straight up. My Mercedes has never had a problem with Haldon Hill – I just squeeze the accelerator and move into the outside lane at the first available opportunity – but lorries and other large vehicles have real difficulty, as do small cars generally. The times I have flashed past boy racers in their rustbuckets, proudly bought with the first pay cheque from their Saturday job, and full of their mates and girlfriends, boom boxes blaring, frowning and swearing as they swallow their pride and change down to second gear or risk stalling – it makes me smile, because that was me, once. Life really is so very short, and at seventeen you have the world at your feet, but you don't see any of that. Youth is wasted on the young, someone once said. I understand the sentiment, but disagree. From there, my thoughts return to Lizzie. I push my foot further to the floor.

Once you reach the apex, the road levels out, and you speed along a fairly straight piece of dual carriageway, which cuts through Haldon Forest. The road climbs again as you turn off for Tamehaven, and then you snake through what feels like moorland at the top of the world. It's a very enjoyable road to drive along, if your vision is not blurred by tears. Eventually there is a sign stating that you have reached 'The Gem of South Devon', and if you look to the right, you see the red Ness jutting out into the open ocean. Then there is another steep descent, and you drop into the little seaside cliché that is Tamehaven.

As I said – a metaphor for life.

I head – as most non-locals do – for the extensive car park that's located where the River Tame becomes the ocean, under the watchful eye – or, rather, nose – of the Ness. I am lucky enough to be able to park right at the front, by the railings. The weather has calmed since the last time I was down this way, and I turn the stereo off and stare into the sparkling, smooth surface of the water until my mood brightens, my professionalism returns, and I begin to feel the sense of accomplishment that I've been striving for. Then I purchase a parking ticket, gather up the notes I have prepared for this evening, walk to the far end of the car park where there's access to the bit of beach opposite the Ness, sit on the warm, sandy sea wall, away from the families who have started their weekend at the first available opportunity, and practise my speech, with the ocean as my audience.

The drive back from the seaside to the university provides me ample time to mentally prepare myself for the evening. After finding the parking space that has been allocated for me, I step out of the car and, enjoying the sensation of what Julia always liked to call 'butterflies' in my abdomen, I stride over to the Princess Alice building with a satisfied smile.

Once I've checked that everything is in place, and greeted everyone who needs to be greeted, I head over to the student bar, the Ram. I go through my notes again, over a Coke, and in true student style, I change into my suit in the toilets. I find myself slightly aroused by the dichotomy in me. My thoughts fly back to Lizzie, admittedly automatically, due to the darkness in me; then I think about where she is and what has happened, and all the secret enjoyment of what can only be described as a midlife crisis is replaced by the knowledge that I wrote the book in order to help people like her. This snaps me back to my professional self – my true self – and I am ready to launch my book. This is my life's work. I am primed for the next phase of my career.

I enter the Princess Alice building from the far side and walk through it, which allows me to see when my guests have taken their seats in the auditorium, rather than walking in through the main door to reception and having them all see me. I think this evening deserves some drama.

My timing is perfect – the reception area is empty, save for one suited man who is just disappearing into the lecture theatre. The heavy between-corridors fire door swings closed behind me with a thud, and his instinctive response to the sound in a room he thought was empty, is to turn and look in the direction of the noise. When his eyes meet mine, they flash and a smile full of hate splits his face. It's Sasha.

"Congratulations," he purrs, as he slides back into the auditorium. "Enjoy your special evening."

Julia

The secret growing in my abdomen keeps my rage in check.
Sasha invited me to the launch of my husband's book,
although we have not arrived at the university together. I don't
know if Erazmus has told any of his colleagues, or indeed any
of our friends, that we are getting divorced, so I will play the
dutiful wife and tell everyone how proud I am of my husband
and his work until I know how the land lies. I doubt Erazmus
has told a soul. I told Sasha, of course, and he was delighted,
but he is not one for gossip in the workplace, or anywhere else;
I am nonetheless relieved when the double doors are opened
by two of the smartly dressed students who have been serving
us all champagne, and I can take my seat in the front row of
the upper section. A rush of love washes through me when I
realise that, in not so many years, I will be in the very front
row at my child's school play. I imagine him or her kneeling in
some straw in the assembly hall, next to a crib with a plastic
baby in it, as Mary or Joseph in the Nativity.

I am enjoying the glow of my daydream so much that,
when Sasha stalks in, I smile warmly at him, and beckon him
to sit next to me. His face lights up when he sees me and,
keeping his eyes locked on mine, he takes his place on my
left, his smile triumphant, but the light in his eyes oddly
malignant.

Seconds after Sasha has settled himself next to me, his
firm thigh encased in fitted tweed pushing delectably against
my leg, my husband strides in – hardback and notes in hand –
with the professional smile of an eminent doctor. Confidence
and authority radiate from him. This is the moment he has
been working for – the pinnacle of his career – and in spite of
everything that had happened in the last few months, I am
filled with pride, happiness, and even love for Erazmus – my

incredibly accomplished husband. The moment ends as quickly as it had begun – Erazmus is surveying us all before he opens his mouth to speak, and I know that he's already planning his next move up the ladder. He's a workaholic; in allowing him to have priority in achieving his heart's desire, I have given away any hope of achieving mine. Sasha presses his thigh closer, and it's as if he can read my mind, and is reminding me that I haven't sacrificed my needs – I am working on it right now, with him, Sasha. I almost told Shirley when she rang the other day, but something made me stop, and I was glad – I want to hold onto my tiny, precious secret for a bit longer, just to nurture it and feed it all my love. Sasha makes to sip his champagne, notices that I don't have a glass, and offers me his. I shake my head, and Sasha's eyes sparkle, and he smiles. A warmth flushes through me – he's pleased I am doing my best for my – our – baby.

Erazmus is talking, and people are clapping, so I smile broadly and join them, as a good wife would. Sasha claps softly – almost silently – with his head cocked a little to the left. He's one of the earliest to stop clapping, and when his hands fall to his lap, one grazes the length of my thigh, and I feel myself blush. That's the point when Erazmus finally picks me out in the crowd. I stop clapping, but smile at him. Erazmus returns my smile, albeit shyly, and opens his mouth to continue his presentation, but then his eyes dart left, and he notices Sasha. His hesitation hadn't been noticed by anyone but me – and probably Sasha – but he pauses and takes a sip of water from the glass on the lectern while glancing down at his notes. I feel myself flush again, but Erazmus is back in professional mode and is making eye contact with everyone in the room except Sasha and myself. I wish I was able to turn my emotions on and off like he can. It's almost mechanical, automatic, robotic – a response ironically, but aptly, innate in him: if something bothers you, switch it off until you have time to deal with it properly. I remember him telling me about the phenomenon of patients blanking out their memories of terrible things that have happened to them. It's a survival technique. Sometimes the memories return – for instance in the form of flashbacks – and sometimes they don't. I am sure that Erazmus is capable of doing this at will.

Suddenly, I'm aware that Sasha has tensed in his seat. I realise I haven't heard a word that Erazmus has been saying. I begin to panic, and wonder if I should pick up someone's drained champagne flute and pretend to be drunk after all. Not so many months ago, Erazmus would have practised this speech with me, as well as things that could potentially come up in the Q and A session that would inevitably follow; now, I have no idea what he's been talking about, what he's about to say, or even what the book is called. How do I not know the title of his book?! Is it *The Blue Octagon*? It must be psychiatry jargon. Sasha puts his right hand firmly over both of mine, making me aware that I've started to pick off the nail polish I just this afternoon applied. I turn slightly towards Sasha, in apologetic embarrassment, but he's staring straight at Erazmus, and although I can only see his profile, I can feel the depth and intensity of the hatred that Sasha is blasting towards my husband. It's actually shocking; and that shock forces me to take in what Erazmus was saying.

Erazmus is expostulating on one of his case studies; one from years ago, involving a teenage girl. He's explaining how at that point in his career, he'd begun to be able to 'tell', like a gut feeling, which of his patients were going to – in any sense of the word – recover, and those who were not. He'd done all he could, he says, to keep the girl in care, in spite of the family interfering, saying that their daughter would be 'better off at home' with them, where they could 'look after her'. In this instance, shortly after the patient had been released, she had drowned herself. Erazmus pauses at this point, and raises his eyebrows. The gesture is almost imperceptible – he's taken another glance down at his notes – but it was there. I saw it. Sasha saw it. Erazmus implied that if the parents had been looking after their daughter properly in the first place, she never would have got to the point where a section had been necessary, and if she had stayed in care, she would have been alive today. And that's when Sasha stands up.

I can actually feel the heat of the hatred radiating off him. Every member of the audience had been silent and absorbed in Erazmus' words throughout, but a deeper hush falls across us all in a wave from the back rows to the front, where Erazmus is already stock-still and silent, staring at Sasha, astounded, but also, I can tell, a little scared.

Sasha waits until every sound in the room has been muffled, as with a blanket of thick snow. I hear him inhale and exhale before pausing and speaking very softly, but with absolute clarity.

"There is a proverb," he begins, addressing the entire auditorium, "'To kill with kindness'. It is commonly used by people when they are talking about over-feeding a companion animal, or over-watering a plant. Sometimes it is used between mothers at the school gate in reference to the eight-year-old who remains unable to tie their own shoes, or zip up their own coat. These are simple things, relatable things, understandable things, forgivable things. Forgivable things.

"Unfortunately, the saying can also describe the behaviours of professional people. Sometimes, as in this case, of healthcare professionals. This is not forgivable.

"Killing with kindness, when done by a professional working in the mental healthcare sector, is laziness. It is laziness, and a complete refusal to look a failing system in the face, and work to change it for the better. In fact, it is unprofessional. It is arrogance. It is negligence. And to then use an instance of this negligence in an attempt to further one's career, to benefit financially from it, and indeed to expect reverence for it, is, frankly, despicable.

"The NHS is in crisis. It has been for a long time, but especially so now. I am not seeking to make a political statement here. I am trying to point out that a failing system can, and should, be changed from within. There is not enough money. Of course, it is far easier to keep an individual under a section than to try to rehabilitate them. Yes, the care, the clothes, the food, the medication, the power, the staffing and running of an institution all cost money. But 'Society' is 'safe' – safe from individuals who have the potential to harm others (but don't we all?); in addition, it is safe from feeling any culpability from the suicides of others. Care in the Community involves an entire team of professionals looking after different aspects of a patient's well-being: from psychotherapists, to pharmacists, to social workers, to the wardens at supported-accommodation sites, to council workers; then to taxpayers, to the neighbours of patients who feel their homes are being devalued, to the untrained but ever-responsible family members of those patients; finally, to their psychiatrists.

"And there, Dr Whittle," Sasha spits, raising his voice a touch, "there, you and I have a problem.

"I assume – although we both know what people say about assumptions – that you are familiar with self-fulfilling prophecy, *Dr* Whittle?"

Sasha pauses, until Erazmus realises that his understudy's question is not rhetorical. The situation has clearly put Erazmus into a state of shock, because he fumbles over words he needn't utter, and says, "Of course."

"And I am also assuming that you are aware of how impressionable those with mental illness can be?"

Erazmus nods. I imagine a fly on the wall, smiling with amusement at the heads of those in the audience turning between Sasha and Erazmus, as if they're watching a game of tennis.

"So, it's fair for me to make another assumption – that when a consultant psychiatrist informs a patient time and again that they are ill and that they need professional help of the kind that can only be found in psychiatric residential accommodation, that that patient will come to believe that the psychiatrist knows best, and that there is no hope for them of ever living a full and productive life; that they will only ever be a waste of space and of oxygen and food and taxpayers' money; that they deserve never to be unsupervised again; that they do not deserve their basic human right – their freedom!"

Sasha's voice grows louder and louder, and as he reaches the end of his monologue, he's almost shouting. Erazmus is motionless at the lectern, his mouth slightly agape. I watch as Sasha inhales and exhales deliberately again. After a pause, he continues, in the cold, quiet, sinister tone he began with.

"It is hard for us 'normal', 'mentally healthy' members of society to believe that there is something worse than losing our freedom. But there is. People talk about 'hopelessness', but very few actually know how it feels to be completely without hope.

"My sister, Amber, or 'Gem', as you so very cleverly disguised her in your book, Dr Whittle, had experienced what it was like to be completely without hope. Can you guess which professional, working within the mental healthcare sector at the time she died, had taken away her hope? It was you, Dr Whittle. You wrote my sister off, until she wrote herself off. It might only be manslaughter if it went to court, but, *Dr* Whittle – you were responsible for her death. You killed her. You killed my sister!"

There's a low gasp, and murmured conversation breaks out. All eyes are fixed on Erazmus, who remains motionless. Sasha, though still standing, is trembling, and his hands have balled into fists. The pause is too long, and the hush descends again. Neither of these powerful, authoritative, charismatic men know what to do. They are both in shock. I am in shock. I am completely numb. I know instinctively that Sasha has spoken the truth.

Erazmus regains his composure first. He starts by slowly shaking his head, and his mouth slides into a thin, tight smile. Very quietly, he says, "I am truly saddened to hear that Amber was your sister, Sasha, and that you've held this awful loss inside for such a terribly long time. However, I can assure you that your sister had indeed been very unwell, and that her death, tragic as it was, was entirely due to her illness. I understand your reasons for apportioning blame to me, but, Sasha, we are both psychiatrists, and are thus acutely aware that laying blame at a doctor's door is a classic response to grief at the death of a loved one. I am sincerely sorry for your loss, but reiterate that I acted – and only ever act – in the best interests of my patients."

Erazmus grows calmer and more controlled with every word he utters, and by the time he's finished speaking, he is master of the room once again. His eyes flick over his audience, and he smiles an apologetic – if slightly patronising – smile, before turning to the security guards I hadn't even noticed were in the room, and whispering "Please" to them, with a small nod in Sasha's direction. The men begin to close in around Sasha, and the one who reaches the end of the aisle in which Sasha and myself had taken our seats, holds his hand out to Sasha, and murmurs, "This way, please, sir," as if he's speaking to a confused elderly person.

Sasha's head whips round ninety degrees, and he glares at the poor young man. The security guard loses his poise, and glances at his colleague for reassurance. The older man frowns at his understudy, who repeats his gentle command, but a touch more loudly.

Now it's Sasha who's shaking his head, and his unusually red lips force themselves into a thin smile.

"This is so typical of the dominant, elitist, commercialist social set-up of England! A younger, more forward-thinking man – a fresh pair of eyes in a stagnant system – comes forward promoting a new idea – a valid, solid, practical idea, that would improve a dated system and be of benefit for staff, patients and families alike – and he is immediately shouted down by the old man with the better job title, and dismissed by everyone!

"Can you not see what your darling Dr Whittle has just done?!" Sasha shouts, spinning around to make eye contact with everyone in the room and accuse them personally. "He told my sister she was ill, without hope, and he's told you that I am also mentally unstable because I am grieving, so my word is ignored too!

"The powerful silence those who would speak out and change things. They like the status quo, because it is the status quo of their making, and they dominate it. This is the same class war that has been raging for centuries! Label dissidents as ill, and you take away their voice! There is a new century approaching, for goodness' sake, and you are all still following the old, inefficient, unfair ways! You are being controlled! Are you all blind to that?!"

But the security guards are working as a team, and the young man restrains Sasha and pulls him out of the aisle before Sasha has finished his monologue. Sasha bends his head, and allows himself to be guided down the stairs. Erazmus is smiling, fully in control of the situation, and the buzz in the audience begins to die away. I am flooded with sadness. In a few months, I will have a child – I am responsible for the world I'm bringing that child into; and it is Sasha's child. I've chosen Sasha over my husband physically, and I'll choose him emotionally, too.

I cry out "Sasha!" and stumble to the end of the aisle, my dress catching on the thick velvet of the seats. Sasha spins his gaze in my direction, and it's as if my eyes fill him with hope and fight again. He smiles widely, with a passion that I choose to interpret as love, and tries to shake himself clear of the young security guard. He's triumphant, and faces Erazmus as I come to a halt slightly behind him. Sasha reaches back his arm, and our hands clasp. All the colour drains out of Erazmus' face. The security guard, Andy, as his name badge declares, lets go of the defector.

"Wha-?" Erazmus begins, but I cut him off.

"Sasha is right, Erazmus. When things aren't working, doing nothing is compliance and weakness. I cannot stand by and watch your obsession with your career ruin any more lives!"

My husband is stunned into silence and stillness for the second time in a matter of minutes.

Self-fulfilling prophecy is working for me! The relief is so overwhelming, I almost cry. An ecstatic sob escapes my lips. "It's over! I love Sasha, Erazmus. We're having a baby!" And I lean into Sasha's shoulder, and wait for his arm to encircle my waist; for him to hug me close and kiss me. He does neither. His whole body goes as stiff as a board. He gives Erazmus a hate-filled smile, and turns it on me.

"Wonderful news, Julia," he spits, and he flings open the double doors and strides out of the auditorium.

Sasha

Unbelievable! I have not decided whether I am furious or elated at the events of this evening; but I have decided that I am the only sane person I know. The cool, damp air strikes me, and the simple act of breathing it in makes me feel better. I take large, deep breaths, sometimes through my mouth, and I'm almost at the corner of the road when I hear the heavy double doors of the Princess Alice building clang shut behind me.

I storm down the hill and out of the university grounds, making my way quickly up the hill and into the city centre. I need a drink. I need several drinks. I need to be somewhere where no one knows or will recognise me. At the park gates, I cross the road onto the college side, and then cross again so that I can walk up Victoria Street and look for a bar. I head for the Angel, but find myself walking straight past it. I could take a train to the coast, at Central Station, but I push onwards until I see a sign for The Coal Mine. The name is familiar to me from the local newspapers – it's that dingy little club where all the supposedly up-and-coming bands play. I laugh when I read the name of the band who are 'headlining' tonight – Charcot! This is where I will spend the evening, then. I am curious as to where the quartet of hair-dye enthusiasts came across the name of their band.

Since I moved back to Devon, and started working at The Meadows, I've relearned what small-town life is like. Pathetic, in a word. The gossip, the hopelessness – it's like that song by Slug, or Pulp or whatever they call themselves, that I keep hearing when I accidentally press the radio button on my car stereo. *Common People*, it's called. There is clearly a problem with the culture of the society here, and in my – admittedly limited – research, the council, police and social services seem to be doing very little to combat it. Some would argue that it's caused by poverty, some that it was the Tory government, some that it's a conspiracy, some that it's simply coincidence. 'There must be something in the water!' is a saying that has been quoted at me numerous times, accompanied by a little giggle. But when you have eight patients on your books who are from the same school, and five of them have been victims of child sexual abuse, carried out by at least four different men of a certain age, you have a cultural problem. I have raised this point at departmental meetings, and have even spoken off the record to a local policeman. I have been fobbed off, every single time. And the venerable Dr Whittle is one of the people who has been most vocal in the fobbing. "Unless the girls come forward, there is nothing we can do." I have countered this argument time and again by stating that three of the men are already dead, and that the girls are scared. And ill. And have no support from anyone, bar our services. And these are the ones who have come to us for help – there must be many more who haven't and are still suffering, or have died. But by this point, no one is listening. There is no proof, only allegations that the alleged victims have made – allegations that none of them are willing to take any further. And they are mentally ill. Psychiatric patients, in practice, have no rights – especially the manic and the delusional. The word of an unlabelled person will be taken over that of one who has been labelled mentally ill, every time. I found this to my cost, with the episode with Kayleigh-Amanda Tarr. I will never forgive myself; but I will never repeat the mistake.

Enough vitriolic obsessing. I am at the entrance to the cut-through which leads to The Coal Mine Club. Many of my patients have spoken about the place. They go there not just because the alcohol is cheap and entrance fee small – they go there to lose themselves in music, with a group of people who are like-minded. Everyone who has mentioned the club has stated that they go there because it feels like home. That they fit in.

I discover that the club is – as its name should have suggested – underground. A metal barrier around the top of a descending, spiral staircase, and a poster and a sandwich board are all that greets you from the top. 'New kids on the indie scene', Charcot, are playing this evening, it announces, and from the noise emanating from the club below, it is packed. A group of teenagers are sitting on the top steps, swigging from bottles. One of them is attempting to light what is clearly a spliff. As I approach, I remove my jacket, undo my tie and push my shirtsleeves above my elbows. The blond adolescent uncups his hand from his face, leaving the spliff dangling from his lips, and flicks a switch on the side of his lighter. An extremely long flame shoots up, causing him to jump back. His three friends laugh at him, and he says with the spliff bobbing in his mouth, "Fuck me! I nearly lost my eyebrows there!" The rolled-up bit at the end of the spliff quickly burns up and drops off. The lad draws on the spliff, raises his eyebrows and splutters a bit. His mates laugh again, as does he. Then he registers me, and cocks his head up to meet my eyes. His are a little bloodshot. He smiles. "You all right, mate?" he asks. "You looked well stressed!"

"Yeah, bad day at the office," I reply, returning the smile, and making to go down the steps to the hatch where a girl who is mostly eyeliner and tattoos and glitter, is taking money. The lads shuffle to the side, and the blond one offers me the spliff.

"Take a couple of tokes on this, mate," he says with a grin. "That'll sort you out."

I thank him, take the badly-rolled joint, and do as he suggests. I have never smoked marijuana before, but I have smoked cigarettes, and I know that etiquette with drugs is that you draw it deep into your lungs and hold it for as long as possible, so this is what I do. It is vile, and I cannot suppress my coughing fit, which induces the lads to laugh again. I am about to hand it back, when the drug – whatever it is – hits my frontal lobe like a brick. It is so powerful that I almost stagger back. And I laugh, pull back my hand and take another pull. This time I gain control, and let the smoke escape from my lips slowly. The lads are watching me, grinning, which makes me laugh again, and the smoke comes out of my nostrils, which hurts like hell, but we are all in hysterics now, so I shake my head, pass the spliff back to the blond lad, and make to go down the stairs.

"Good idea, mate," the blond lad says. "The band will be on in a minute."

Erazmus

The doors of the auditorium hiss softly as they slowly close behind Sasha. I imagine he wanted them to slam. There is silence in the room. I am holding my notes, staring at the doors. I am frozen for the third time in less than an hour. I wish this peace would last forever, so I could stay numb, and the consequences of Sasha's outpouring be perpetually delayed; but in the act of thinking this, the chaos floods in. Julia has run the short distance between us, and is clenching my upper arms, shaking me, trying to get the reaction she wants: immediate forgiveness and assurance. After a few seconds, I am unable to avoid making eye contact with her. Her face is a blubbery mess of tears, mascara and snot, and is far too close to my own. She is trying to make me understand something, although her speech is impeded by her tears and emotion. Now she is calling my name, over and over, between sobs that would, in other circumstances, be heart-wrenching. I am repulsed by the heat of her breath, and I push her away. The security guards are looking sheepish so, breaking away from Julia's gaze, I ask the nearest one if he can escort my wife to somewhere quiet. He guides her out of the room, and I dismiss her from my mind, and turn to address my audience. Most of them are standing, and some have moved into small groups. It is so painfully clear that no one knows what to do or how to behave, that I give a small laugh, and clear my throat. Silence descends, and I gesture for them to be seated. Like puppets, they do so.

"Well!" I begin, and smile, passing my gaze over the filled seats, and letting them rest on the only two empty ones. "That was unexpected! If anyone would like to leave at this point, I will understand completely, but I do have a few words to say." No one moves. I wonder how much of it is solidarity, and how much is rubber-necking curiosity.

"Thank you. Of course, I cannot go on with this evening in the way I intended and pretend nothing untoward has happened here. However, I would like to say that, as with most things in life, and especially at this time in our history, things are changing – as is only natural – and differing thoughts and perspectives are coming to the fore. We are approaching a new millennium. But I will state, here and now, that I have never acted with anything less than complete professionalism, and a duty of care to my patients and the society in which they live. I have many, many years of training, practising, treating and teaching behind me, and I intended with this book to give an overview of it, so that others could gain insight into the profession, and that studies can be done in order to improve our service, and forward our techniques and treatments, as well as understanding the unique nature in which patients with the same diagnosis can experience that illness. My intention with writing was to add to the scientific data, the community, and the help for the mentally ill.

"It is with great regret and sadness that in the last few weeks, events in my personal life have detracted from my life's work, but, I suppose, that is life, and the way we choose to deal with situations of this nature is what defines us as people. I choose to face this as I have every other scenario in my life – with professionalism and good grace.

"I will now close what remains of this presentation. I will sit in the reception area with a coffee until the planned finishing time of this event. Anyone who wishes to talk with me about my book, *The Blue Octopus – Redefining Sanity*, is very welcome. I will be back in my office at The Meadows on Monday morning. Thank you for your time."

I step down from the lectern to a smattering of applause which quickly gains momentum. As I turn away, I notice that there is no one who is not clapping. The relief is almost overwhelming.

A student offers me a glass of champagne as I move over

to the worn, brown leather seats of the comfy reception chairs. I smile at her, take it, and choose the seat which is at the far end of the area. Scanning the room, I am exceedingly glad to find that Julia is nowhere to be seen. The student has been watching me, and says, "Your wife left a few minutes ago, Dr Whittle." I thank her again, shuffle my notes and sit down. My colleagues, along with guests I don't recognise, are heading in my direction. Most have sympathetic smiles. "Aren't you going to try to find your wife?" the student asks. I had no idea she was still standing next to me. This is impertinence, and I look her full in the face in an attempt to both remember where I have seen her before, and to read her expression and thus ascertain her intention, but Phee Canonteign glides over in an invisible cloud of patchouli oil, and lifts a flute of champagne from the student's silver tray. Her habitual oversized earrings swing so violently as she turns to face me, that I wonder her earlobes don't tear. She smiles at me, and then widens it as she turns to make eye contact with the student, before stepping in front of her, and effectively dismissing her.

It is always best to expect the unexpected – or, rather, to expect nothing at all. It's one of the great ironies of our evolution – our ability to plan and assess, so that we can react in the most opportune manner for us to get the outcome we desire, and thus reduce stress, can inversely be the thing that causes us stress. I believe that if we could only live in the moment a bit more, in the way that animals do, we would stop all this unnecessary brain ache. I've looked forward to and planned for this evening for years, and though at one point I'd thought it was turning into an unmitigated disaster that would herald the end of my career, things actually conclude very well. The response from my audience is positive, and sales from my book reach over one hundred; some copies are purchased by the students who are serving us drinks.

I feel good as I thank the university staff and the inebriated stragglers, and walk out into the cool, damp air, back to my car. Although the evening had, for several reasons, demanded a glass of champagne, I'm glad I otherwise abstained. I can enjoy this moment with a clear head, and in the morning plan properly how I'm going to deal with Julia when I next see her. In spite of my anger at her for committing adultery with the only human in the world I despise, I'm being slowly crushed by sadness. Our divorce will quickly come – we've both transgressed – and now we are both free to pursue our own versions of happiness.

But there's more to it than that. The fact that Julia slept with someone else hurts like hell – and I know I'm a hypocrite. The situation is farcical, and so bittersweet that saltwater stings my eyes. I would have let the tears fall, but I'm aware of quick, light footsteps behind me, and I blink them back as a female voice calls my name. I stop to let the young woman catch up; it's the dark-haired student with the nose stud who had been so impertinent earlier.

"Dr Whittle!" she calls again, slightly breathlessly when she's a few metres in front of me. "Thank you for waiting! I'm sorry – I need to apologise for being so rude before. I – I have a million reasons, and I think the shock of it all had something to do with it, but I am sorry, and I wondered if I could talk to you for a minute. If you have time?" the girl trails off and drops her gaze to the pavement. She flicks her grey eyes up again briefly before dropping them once more, with a shy, apologetic smile.

"Of course! And I should be the one apologising for rudeness, really – for letting my colleague barge you away like that."

The girl smiles and gives a small laugh. "That's okay."

I let the pause hang while I return her smile, wondering who she is, waiting for her to explain why she's come after me. She stumbles over her words.

"Umm, I'm a nurse, but I'm studying psychology here – I'm in my first year – and when I saw you were launching your book here, I volunteered to help – just to see what I could learn from you – from you all – and then maybe I thought I could get a copy of your book? I really am very interested in reading it – although I know I'm nowhere near that level yet. You've kind of inspired me."

I've unlocked my car and am scrabbling about on the back seat for spare copies before she's finished her sentence, and hold one up as she does so. Her face lights up, and she reaches out her hand to take it before saying, "Oh, goodness, I almost forgot – how much is it?" rummaging in the rainbow-coloured knitted bag slung over her left shoulder.

I shake my head. "No, no, don't worry about that – you've been helpful at the event this evening, and I'm guessing they didn't pay you much for your troubles?"

"Umm, no," she replies. "It was a voluntary thing."

"Well, that's just cemented my decision," I tell her. "In fact, if you tell me your name, I'll even sign it for you!"

"Oh my goodness, would you?!"

"Of course!" I say, opening the book to the dedication page, and pulling my Parker pen from the inside pocket of my suit jacket. There's a pause, while I gaze at her, waiting for her to tell me her name. Her manner is endearing, and somehow familiar.

"Oh, sorry, you want my name! It's Sally. Sally Whiley."

I pause before writing my dedication to her and ask, "Do you have a brother?"

Julia's Audi is parked in what used to be its place on the drive. My heart sinks. I'm exhausted. It's typical of her to panic – I should have expected that she'll want a resolution tonight. Why can't she just go back to her flat and let us all sleep on this?! It occurs to me that she could have been lying about having rented a place of her own – she's probably been shacked up with Sasha, and I think everyone who'd been in the auditorium knows that Sasha had walked out of more than just the hall when he'd exited earlier. I berate myself for feeling slightly amused by this. Julia is my wife, and we had been desperately in love, once. We had been, hadn't we? I wouldn't have married her otherwise. Would I? And now she is carrying a child, and stress is not conducive to a healthy pregnancy. And one life has already been lost to this mess. Speculation is not productive.

I get out of the car as if I've just returned home from a normal working day, unlock the front door, walk directly into the kitchen and straight to the kettle, which I fill and set to boil. I can hear the floorboards creaking above, then Julia hurrying down the stairs. She rushes into the kitchen and catches me in a bear hug before I have time to react. She's saying my name over and over. Her face is blotchy, and there are black streaks down her cheeks where tears have taken her mascara and dried. She's cried herself out. She's scared. I hold her by her upper arms and rub them until she calms down. Then I wait.

"Erazmus. I am so, so sorry. I – I – my hormones are all over the place, and I was angry, and I – I lied about the baby being Sasha's," she begins.

I'm about to cut her off before she takes this ludicrous lie any further, but my wife puts a finger over my lips, and speaks over me.

"I'm not going to deny that I slept with him – I did, while you were away, because I was so angry and hurt and confused and I wanted to hurt you, and then when you came back and things seemed to be okay, I didn't want to wreck things by telling you, and then tonight – well, my hormones are all over the place, and I – well I said what I said, but the baby is yours, Erazmus. I was pregnant before you went away – I just hadn't said anything – and then I wanted to hurt you, so …".

"Julia! Stop this ridiculous monologue! The child isn't mine. You know it isn't mine, and there is a scientific reason it isn't mine – I am infertile! I am physically unable to father a child!"

Her reaction shocks me. My wife is immediately cold and controlled. She looks at me with such hatred, I feel as though she's actually punched me. She's saying something, but I don't catch it.

"Pardon? Julia, what did you say?"

"I said, 'You knew?!'" Then she turns, very deliberately, walks to the porch, picks up her handbag, and goes out. I hear her rev the Audi hard before she speeds away.

Julia

I drive out to Sasha's house. I want to know where I stand by the morning, so I can focus on how I'm going to raise my child. I have a pretty good idea of what he'll say, but I need to hear it from his lips, one on one. I know he doesn't want our baby. I think about calling Shirley. But if I'm going to speak with her, I need to have all the facts so that we won't go round in circles, speculating, so I continue driving along the twisting, pot-holed lanes to Sasha's house. It's completely dark, except for the stars and my headlights – as soon as the white lines disappear from the centre of the roads, so too do the streetlights. The hedges close in on either side, and I hope to goodness that I don't meet another car – I've never been great at reversing, and how on earth are you supposed to reverse if there's no light behind you, and you don't know where the last passing point is? I go cold all over, and realise that I'm huddled up against the steering wheel, as if that will give me a better view, and that my hands have started to sweat. I curse myself for not paying more attention on my previous journey, but just when my chin starts to shake and I'm about to cry, I spot the stone bearing the name of Sasha's house. The tears come then, but they're of relief.

My tyres crunch over the stony driveway, and I stop by a wall. It isn't until I cut the engine and flick the headlights off that I realise there are no lights on in Sasha's house; the whole place is really creepy. My heart doesn't want to admit that I know he isn't at home, so I turn the key in the ignition without starting up the engine, and switch the lights back on. I am scared, angry and hurt. I feel ill, and realise I'm now sweating all over. I need to get inside, but the front door is locked, so I walk as far around the building as the light from

153

my car reaches, and peer into the darkened windows. There are no lights on anywhere, and it's so still that I can hear the occasional flap of bat wings, and the intermittent hooting of some kind of owl. I return to my car, perch on the bonnet and let the tears fall. Where the fuck is Sasha? And then it strikes me that he had seemed a little drunk at the university. He'd been drunk and reckless – of course, he's gone to a pub! He's got a meeting at The Beeches in the morning, which is annoying because it means we can't meet for coffee, but I know that won't stop him. He's one of those men who finds solace at the bottom of a bottle. Like he did when the leaflets on pregnancy that Faye Farefield had given fell out of my bag the other day. He'd left me on my own all night. But then when he'd returned, it had been bliss! The conflicting emotions are so strong that I get a wave of nausea, and I find I am humming that piano piece by Rachmaninoff to steady myself until it passes.

When I feel better, I remember that I still have one of Sasha's CDs. I stand to make my way over to my car, to play it. Suddenly, there's a terrible, harsh scream from somewhere out in the darkness. It makes me scream, too, and I jump back into the car, slamming the door, and punching all the little black sticks that lock the doors from the inside. I crunch myself up in the driver's seat, wishing I hadn't let out that scream, and brace myself, my heart racing, my breath coming in gulps, while I process that the sound I'd heard hadn't been human. Another bout of sickness hits me, and for a second, I'm reminded of that Sherlock Holmes story that had scared me so much as a child, *The Hound of the Baskervilles,* and I almost scream again. 'I am a mother now, I have to be strong,' I reprimand myself, and I peek out of the windscreen, notice the bushes in front of my car shake, and then a dark shape emerges – I hold my breath until I realise it's a fox. Just a bloody fox! I have to get out of here. I sob, and am about to turn the key in the ignition before I acknowledge the stupidity and futility of driving back to Exeter on the off-chance that I'll see Sasha lurching between bars, and I don't want to go back to my flat because that will mean I'll only have to come back and try to find him later on. Sobs wrack me again, and after a while I turn the lights off so as not to waste the car battery, and climb into the back. I'm incredibly thirsty and haven't brought a drink, and I need the toilet, but have nowhere to go. I shut my eyes and hope that exhaustion will carry me off to sleep for a few hours, but a strange thought pops into my head out of nowhere, and I sit up, laughing. Drinks. Snacks. Toilet stops. Entertainment. These things will become paramount to my journeys in a handful of months! And what name shall I choose for my baby?

What I really need is to be out of this altogether. My thoughts run to taking a sabbatical, and I laugh at the irony. I think about what Sasha said at the book launch. The very fact that the girl in question was Sasha's sister means that he's compromised, professionally. And an awful lot of people have been up in arms about Care in the Community. But Erazmus has always said that it should be taken on a case-by-case basis, and the right decision made for the right patient, but ultimately, someone has to make the final call, and someone has to fund it. And psychiatrists are only human – they make mistakes, too. It's just that the consequences of their perceived errors are more far-reaching than me forgetting that our classroom is down to its last bottle of red paint the Friday before Valentine's Day. But that's why psychiatrists get paid so much. But one of the things that attracted me to Erazmus was that he had empathy, and he wanted to help people and make a difference. He wouldn't have wanted to section a young girl unless he thought that there was a real danger to herself and/or others. The fact of the matter was that she did end up killing herself, and no one but her will ever know the truth behind that act. But then isn't that element of his nature the very reason that he got in all that trouble over Elizabeth? And I don't know how to define what happened between us the last time we had sex. How well do I know my husband, really? How well do I know Sasha, really? I wonder if I'm the one having the midlife crisis, and then I remember that I'm pregnant. Whatever I do, I have to make the right choice for my child. And then I remember why I had finally walked out on Erazmus. My stomach begins to cramp. He'd always known that he couldn't father a child. It wasn't just that he didn't want them – he couldn't have them. He should have been honest with me. I think I'm going to be sick – the stress of all this is making me ill. I'd felt so guilty for years – years! – that if I pushed for what I wanted, I'd be going back on my word. He'd lied to me. It was worse than lying. It was not telling the whole truth. More cramps – I must calm myself for my baby – I need some painkillers. I wonder what else Erazmus has not been truthful about. I have to get home, take some ibuprofen, get a glass of water, go to bed. I'll feel better in the morning. I'm crying. I'm shivering. I'm back at square one.

I let out an involuntary sob – I am being tortured both mentally and physically – I turn the key in the ignition, sit as comfortably as I can, and pull away from Sasha's house.

I drive through tears, waves of nausea, terrible, terrible pain. I am spasming in agony as I struggle out of the car, push open my door. Cramps are now wracking my body. I stagger to my bathroom. My clothes are soaked with blood. The toilet bowl fills with blood. I pass something, and crawl to the floor. I watch my hands pull me up so I can look in the toilet – purplish clumps of something sinking into vermillion liquid. I can't make it to the telephone, all I can do is cry and cry out, and I know I have lost our baby. My baby.

Sasha

I have never met a more stupid woman in my life. She must know I have access to medication. She must know that I can prescribe whatever I like to whomever I like, and even go and collect it for them. Mifepristone, and then six to seventy-two hours later, Misoprostol, and as much Doxycycline as I can get into her. She doesn't know. She knows that pregnancy can alter the sense of taste. And she does know that, having lost my baby after all I have done for her, I am heartbroken and unable to continue our relationship. And I am free. I will avenge you, Amber. I swear it.

Erazmus

My worry for Julia lasts about twenty minutes. I make some coffee, pace the kitchen floor, consider ringing Shirley; then I switch to pragmatism. Julia is too emotional to be able to hold a constructive conversation, and our divorce is in progress. The thought occurs to me that I should make a return visit to Swansburne and take some more holiday, but I really need to stay on top of my work at The Meadows, and deal with any fallout from the allegations made by Sasha this evening. On the basis of the response immediately after his outburst, I really don't think I have anything to worry about – in fact I hope that Sasha will be the one suffering the consequences. It doesn't help his case that neither him nor any of his family lodged a complaint about me at the time; it doesn't help his case that he made an unprofessional, drunken spectacle of himself in front of his colleagues. My professional self wonders if he would benefit from some bereavement counselling, and I actually make a note to speak to Phee about it in the morning. If he hasn't already resigned. Or been struck off.

Dom

I feel like I'm tripping or something. I heard them. I came downstairs for a cigarette out by the pond like Lizzie and I used to do, thinking that everyone would be either in bed or inside watching the telly, falling asleep in the armchairs, but Heather and Bonnie were out there. They weren't sitting on the chairs by the pond – they were over by the fire escape, and I think Bonnie was about to get in her car to go home. I think they thought they'd be out of earshot, but they weren't.

Lizzie was in hospital – I knew that; we all knew that. But no one else knew that she had my baby inside her. Except, was it my baby? Heather sounded quite severe, like she was telling Bonnie off. Like Bonnie should have seen it coming because she was Lizzie's keyworker. Like Bonnie should have known that Lizzie was having a relationship with Dr Whittle. I fucking knew it. I'll fucking kill him. Because I know in my heart that the baby inside Lizzie is mine, not his. Ugh. He's an old perv, taking advantage, and she thinks she loves him, because he's a professional, he's stable, he has a job and a house and loads of money. With him, she'll be secure. With him, she'll be bored shitless. We've always had a connection, me and Lizzie; she was always in love with me, even when I was with Rebecca. When they carted her off to hospital that day, from the halfway house in Swansburne, I should have gone with her. I should have made her a cup of tea when she was up in her room with her heart and her mind breaking. I should have run after the car that took her away. But I didn't, because Rebecca was holding my hand so tightly, and I knew it would be the end of her if I let go then. She thought we had a connection because of our illness, but we didn't, because an illness is an illness, not a personality quirk. Rebecca never cared about art or music, she just cared about me – but she didn't really, because she didn't care about my art. But would Lizzie really ever have been able to know what it's like to have other people talking in your head? Like, real people who don't even look or sound like you, and they come in and you don't know how they got in, or why they are there, or why you sometimes can't even see them, or why they are saying the things they are saying, to you, of all the people in the world. I think about the psychiatrists – it must be so easy for them, because they've never experienced it, so they are separate and can look at things 'rationally', but they can't ever know what it's like. I wonder if there are any 'recovered' schizophrenic psychiatrists. I hope there are, but I bet they operate undercover. And how would they ever know if they were having a relapse? I guess there are tests and stuff before they get the job. It seems ironic to me – but then I suppose there are the hearing voices groups and all that shit I wish I didn't have to get involved with. Much easier to just get drunk and hold hands with Rebecca. Except she thought we were going to get married. And does it even matter that Lizzie doesn't know what it's like to have other people in her head?

Anyway, Lizzie is going to The Beeches, they reckon. That's the thing about most women, I've found – they can't keep anything in, and they speak more loudly than they think.

I didn't spark up the cigarette – although I really needed one. I just slipped back inside, stuffed some stuff in my rucksack, and crept back out of the door. Bonnie and Heather were still bitching about Dr Whittle – about how they always thought he knew how good looking he was. But they hadn't noticed Dunstan and Lydia. I would have said something, but they'd never believe me, because I'm schizo. But it's too late anyway – I'm already halfway down the hill into town.

The glow from the streetlights is a lurid orange, and although things are quiet up on the hill in the residential area, I can hear the whoops and drunken laughs and shouts from the town centre. Bishopsham is a shithole, but I still feel a rush of excitement when I finally reach the bottom of the hill.

There are groups of teenagers mucking about on the benches; smoking, laughing, looking like they'll spit on you if you look at them wrong. There are homeless guys in their sleeping bags in the sheltered entrances to the shops. There are groups of lads swigging from plastic bottles as they stomp from pub to pub. There are groups of girls pretending not to shiver, stalking about in high heels and tiny dresses, returning the eyeing-up the lads give them as they pass each other. I just about manage to stop myself going in one of the pubs. Even the White Lightning the lads are swigging smells good to me, and the greasy chips in their piss-coloured polystyrene trays, and, if I'm brutally honest with myself, I could do with a shag. But I know I have to get out of Bishopsham before anyone realises I'm gone. It starts to drizzle, and I jog the rest of the way to the station, and can't believe my luck when I find the next train to Exeter is just about to leave.

The line from Bishopsham to Exeter runs right along the coast between Tamehaven and Swansburne, and then up the Exe estuary beyond Starcross until the river disappears for a bit, and you see it for the last time just before the train pulls into Exeter St Davids. I get off at Central, though, and as soon as I've climbed the steps up to Victoria Street, I lose my resolve. The city centre is packed – people all over the place, some of them dressed up – and I follow a group of lads over the road and into a pub called the Angel. I'm actually in a pub for the first time in I don't know how long! I order a cider and sit on a stool at the corner of the bar. The music is great, but so loud it's disorienting. I sit there smiling, and ask the lone guy sat next to me if I can scab a rollie. His eyes are glazed – I'm not sure if it's just the alcohol – and he asks if I'm going to see this up-and-coming indie band, Charcot, who are playing at The Coal Mine. Apparently, everyone else is, including him, so I say, "Yeah, 'course," before I remember I've heard that name before. In fact, haven't I seen them somewhere before?

It turned out I had seen them before in some crumby little shithole of a pub somewhere. Manchester, probably. The bloke gives me a flyer, and I remember the look of the four of them. The Coal Mine is packed. It's underground, so it would have been hot anyway, but the sheer amount of sweating bodies in the queue for the bar, combined with the low red ceiling and the incredibly loud warm-up band, make it feel like one of Dante's circles of hell. Except it's great. It's buzzing. There are candles stuck in wine bottles on all the tables, but all the seats are taken. I can smell weed, too, and automatically start scanning the room for obvious stoners, or dealers. Me and the bloke do a few tequila slammers before everything starts going a bit sparkly and weird, and I feel like I'm being watched. I'm spinning out.

"Mate, I'm going outside for a bit of air," I tell the loner bloke.

"All right. But they'll be on in a bit!" he slurs.

I squeeze and "excuse me" my way towards the exit, and back up the spiralling steps to the little cut-through between Victoria Street and Phoenix Lane. I pass some office bod with thick glasses on the stairs, and I'm sure he looks at me funny. I also get the bad luck fear that I've passed someone on the stairs. Things are getting sketchy, and I realise I haven't taken my meds, that I haven't got them with me, and that if I want to stay incognito, I won't be able to get hold of any. Fuck. There are a group of lads laughing at the top of the steps. One of them is holding a spliff. It's the guys from the band.

"Haha, here comes another one!" the blond guy holding the spliff laughs to the others. "Mate, you need a toke on this!" he says. "It feels good, doing my bit for the community," he laughs. I'm spinning out, but I smile, and take the spliff he's offered.

"Cheers," I say, drawing in a lungful. It's strong as fuck, and absolutely the worst thing I can do for my mental health, but I need the escape. I hold the smoke inside for as long as I can, and let it out slowly through my nose.

My eyes water and sting, but I feel warm and cosy, like I've been wrapped up in cotton wool, in a safe place where nothing bad can get to me. I sit down with the lads, and we pass the spliff around until it's gone, and I'm enjoying having a laugh with these nutters. We're talking about music and art, and I tell them about the stuff I used to do, and they seem really interested, and I end up trying to recreate the one I'd shown to Lizzie, on the inside of an unfolded Rizla packet, with a biro.

"Mate, do you reckon you could do the artwork for our next EP?" says the one with the blue hair, who's picked up one of the loose Rizlas and has almost finished skinning up again, but I never get to say anything, because the bloke I'd met in the Angel comes out and shouts that they're on in ten, and cocks his head to gesture them inside.

"Hang around after the gig – we'll have a drink and sort something out," the blue-haired lad calls up to me from the bottom of the steps. "Oh, and you might as well finish this!" he grins, throwing the fat, hastily rolled spliff back up to me. I catch it with a laugh.

I almost, almost spark it up, but I don't. Doing that sketch had made me remember what I was doing here – trying to find Lizzie, and the fear and the anger and the sadness runs through me, and it clears my mind a bit, because I realise that I can't do anything tonight. I have to get to The Beeches and get inside in the morning, in visiting hours. I can't camp outside the hospital all night; I don't like the idea of spending the night on the drizzly streets of Exeter; and I don't have enough money for a B&B. I think about trekking down to the youth hostel, but if the staff at The Stables realise I'm AWOL, youth hostels will be the first places they'll start looking – then the streets. I carefully pull the joint out of my jeans pocket, let it rest in my open hand, and smile at it. The best thing I can possibly do this evening is to watch the band, stick around after, and hopefully crash wherever they do. I can freshen up in the public loos in the morning and get a bus out to the hospital. So I might as well smoke this joint.

Erazmus

Dominic Whiley has absconded. I call Heather as soon as Sasha leaves my room. Why on earth aren't I the first to know?! He's my patient! He's my patient, and I've let him down. But is this a simple patient-doctor issue? No. Not in this case. It's jealousy. A man-to-man fight for a woman.

Lizzie's baby isn't mine. We never had intercourse. I hadn't been lying when I'd stated that at my disciplinary. And even if we had, her baby still can't be mine – I'd been told long ago that it is "highly unlikely" that I'll be able to father a child – a fact that Faye Farefield is able to corroborate. So Lizzie's baby is not mine. But neither is Julia's. If, indeed, she's pregnant. I feel like I don't know my wife any more. But had I ever known her?

I stand as near as I can to the little rectangular window in my office. There's a small table blocking my way. I placed the table there many years ago, in order that my patients can reach for tissues whenever they want to, or can put things down on it, make notes, or even, as in Dominic Whiley's case, smash it with their fists in frustration. Glancing down from the view of the roofs of the lower hospital departments, across the strip of grass, and over the busy road to the industrial park, I regard the table. It's small, and not exactly sturdy – a cheap pine affair that I bought from MFI years ago. It might seem strange, buying furniture for my own office, but that's what it is – *my* own office; and that's why it hurt so much when that usurper, Grosvenor, had been tossed the keys without a second thought. My office. My office, for which Lizzie had bought me a plastic cactus. I haven't put it back on display since I've been reinstated, but I have kept it in my jacket pocket with my pager. I gently take it out, and even though I know there's no one else in the room, I glance around before I put it to my lips and kiss it. My pager beeps as I place the cactus back in its rightful place on the table that holds the tissues. Simultaneously, the phone on my desk rings.

Within minutes, I'm back in my car, and speeding down the M5. Dominic hasn't been found, but there was a possible sighting of him in a nightclub in Exeter last night. And then in the last few minutes, there's been a mass stabbing in Exeter – just outside the entrance to The Beeches. My mind races; my every thought revolving around Lizzie. Did Dominic presume Lizzie was at The Beeches, and go to find her? Did he have a psychotic episode and stab everyone when he realised she isn't there? Is he on his way to the main hospital? I have to make sure Lizzie is safe.

I literally screech to a stop in the nearest staff car park to the main entrance, and run along the corridors and up the many flights of stairs to the ward on which Lizzie is being treated. I rush to her bed. There's a shadow showing through the curtains. There's someone else in there. It must be Dominic. I try to calm myself, to gather my thoughts. Handling a psychotic young man hell-bent on a purpose shouldn't be attempted alone, but I have no choice. I hear the high-pitched tone of a monitor and throw myself into the room. The person standing over Lizzie is not Dominic.

When I scream her name and she spins round, Julia's face is blank. It's as if I've interrupted her in the middle of washing the dishes. I yank her away from Lizzie and throw her to the floor. Lizzie has flatlined – all I can hear is the continuous screech of the monitor. I've shocked her with the defib and am screaming for help before I know what I'm doing. The curtains are thrust open, there are nurses everywhere, and I am pulled away. Julia is standing motionless and vacant, restrained by a security guard. Lizzie is even paler, her lips tinged with blue.

"What the FUCK have you done?!" I implore Julia, over and over, until I find myself slumped in a low chair, sobbing in a family room, with a nurse I recognise but can't name, handing me a cup of tea.

I have choices. I can let Julia go to prison, or I can beg one of my colleagues to diagnose her with PTSD – thus ending our careers for a woman I am in the process of divorcing; which translates to taking two extremely well-respected psychiatrists out of a struggling health service, and letting down countless struggling patients, for old times' sake. Or I could kill myself, in the hopes that my atheist beliefs turn out to be truths. I have access to all and any drugs under the sun. It would be easy. I sit in that low chair, watching a skin form on the top of my cold, sugary tea, and for the first time in my life, I really do understand the appeal. I'm still waiting for the police to finish their work at the hospital; I'm still waiting to find out if Lizzie is alive or dead. I'm still waiting for the period of numbness that many of my patients attest to have experienced after a traumatic event. I shake my head, and laugh at myself for the judgemental thought that passes through my mind – I'm not that kind of guy. I'm not the 'sort' of person who would kill myself. I lean back in the chair for what must have been the first time in hours, because my spine clicks and my muscles spasm. I stand up and stretch, then swallow the insipid tea in one gulp. I look out of the castle-like slit windows of the family room and see nothing but the door to a store cupboard, and a length of scuffed corridor wall on either side. The architect positioned this room well – I'm being kept away for my own protection, and so that the professionals on duty can do their jobs. But I'm not a prisoner. And I have some training in emergency medicine – perhaps I can help now that I'm calm.

I slowly retrace my steps to the ward. Some nurses are back at the station, scrawling names on the whiteboard so everyone knows who's in which bed. It flashes through my mind that if this wasn't the standard practice, Julia would not have been able to find Lizzie so easily. But then neither would the nurses. Lizzie's name is not there. Either they've moved her to another part of this hospital, transferred her to a new hospital, or she's dead and on a gurney outside the morgue. Bile rises in my throat at the thought, and I push it down. There's a stainless-steel water fountain between a filing cabinet and the porter's trolley, and fighting my repulsion, I bend down and run the tepid water over my mouth and face, and then each hand separately. I stand, but realise that, yes, I am actually so thirsty that I'll drink from a public fountain. I do so, and immediately feel better.

I peer round the corner and into the ward. The bay that Lizzie had occupied is full of police – the forensic team, I presume, and the other patients have their curtains pulled around them. They haven't been moved – I guess there aren't beds to spare. I can hear murmured conversation from behind the curtains, and watch shadows and shapes move behind the flimsy material. I wonder if, and when, the powers that be are planning to replace those curtains. Illustrated with all the so-called sights Exeter has to offer, including the cathedral, the museum and the football ground, with roads connecting them, I find them abhorrent. If the artist had been a child who'd won a competition, there'd be some kind of sentimental value, or even hope, attached, but no, someone cheap had been commissioned to do this. It was the compromise the NHS made between homeliness, practicality, and cost-effectiveness. The background to the design was that grey-green that reminds me of the smell of hospital lunches.

The thought of food – any food – sets my stomach growling; I can't remember when I last ate. I don't know where to look, or what to do. My pager beeps in my pocket – Dominic has been apprehended at The Beeches. This can't be happening.

I turn to exit the ward and make my way to the psych unit, when I feel a heavy hand on my shoulder.

"Dr Whittle?"

"Yes?" I face the tanned and wizened visage of the police officer.

"Dr Whittle, would you mind if I asked you some questions relating to the events of today?" Without waiting for an answer, he guides me back along the corridor to the family room, where a young, blonde officer smiles, introduces herself and gestures for me to sit down. The older officer plonks himself down beside her, opposite my squashy chair, and both of them smile politely when I acquiesce. The female officer produces a notepad and pen, and her superior opens his crinkly old mouth to speak. I cut him off, rising to my feet.

"I'm dreadfully sorry, officers, but my wife has just tried to kill a patient of mine, there has been a stabbing outside the psychiatric unit, and another of my patients has been apprehended there – I really must be there to …"

"No. No, you really must not be there, Dr Whittle," he states. The nurse I'd seen earlier opens the door a fraction, and whispers into the gap, "Teas all round?"

And then I realise where I've seen the nurse before. She hadn't been a nurse when I last saw her. She had been at my book launch. It was Sally Whiley. When she hands me my tea, she murmurs, "Please look after my brother – it's not his fault he's ill!"

Dom

Will's here! I don't know why he's here, because Charcot are a bit heavy for him. A bit 'stadium rock', he'd say. In fact, I think he does say. So I don't know why he's here, because he's more of a plinky-plonky guitar band in a pub where they sell real ales; but he is here, and I don't think he was here to start with, because all I remember to start with is the loner bloke who I cadged a cigarette off, who turned out to be the band's manager, and then smoking that spliff with the boys. The blond one gave me a toke on the spliff, and then the one with the red hair gave me a whole one. I think. But who had the blue hair, then? Will has red hair at the moment, so it might have been him. I used to have red hair. Not any more. The band are really good. Really loud, jumping around, and at the end they all smash their guitars through the bass drum. Lots of guitar solos, quite dark stuff, though. Minor chords and that. It's too heavy for Will. But he has the coke. That's why he's here – he has the baggies! After the gig, no one goes home. There's lots of tequila, salt, lemon and limes. Like that song. And then we're trudging through the streets, but nowhere's open, and we go through this graveyard, and some of them lie on the dead people, but I don't; I go upstairs and it's quite dark and messy and not much furniture except for a battered old petrol-blue leather sofa and a few pine chairs and one bed and some sleeping bags on the floor, and all the cups have coffee dregs in them, and I have to rinse one out to get a drink of water because I'm so thirsty. There's music playing really loud. There's all these dress-up clothes, costumes, comics. There're guitars propped up in corners, and bits of drum kit all over the place, and there's a massive fish tank full of colourful fish with frilly bits, and someone's

169

made some cookies, and some of us are in the sleeping bags, smoking and drinking WKDs, and eating these cookies and watching the fish, and I try to make up a soap opera for the fish like Lizzie had done all that time ago and people were laughing, but I think they're laughing at me, not what I'm saying, and then Will's here again, and some girls are dancing in the front room, and one of them takes all her clothes off and I think she has sex with some of the lads and maybe another girl too; but at one point she beckons me over, and I go over to her and kiss her and ask her what her name is and she tells me it's Lizzie, and I say "You're not Lizzie," and she keeps saying that she is, and keeps trying to grab me, and she's making me angry, and I'm shouting that Lizzie is in the tree place and I have to find her, and then Will is here, and he leads me away and makes me a coffee, but he does a couple more lines while the kettle's boiling, and then we're in the room with the bed but no one's asleep in it because everyone's in the other room with the girls and the frilly fish; and when Will finds out about Lizzie, he takes off his glasses, although he never used to wear glasses, but maybe it's all the intricate artwork he's doing, it's strained his eyes, anyway he says I should hang on to her and never let her go, especially to some wanker who's lied to her and treated her like shit, even if he is loaded – especially if he's loaded, and older. Will says he's lost a girl with a baby to a wanker, and he blamed her for a bit, but it hadn't really been her fault because she had been treated so badly by all these other guys, and she had a baby. He says he's going to play the long game and get her back because he knows she loves him really, and not this other guy, and I ask him how he knows she loved him, and he says that when someone loves you like that you just know, and that makes sense to me, because I've known that Lizzie's loved me for years, but she's in hospital now and I have to find her because she has a baby too and it's mine, and Will asks me when I last took my meds and if I'm feeling okay, and I tell him I am, so he says, "Right. This is what you need to do."

I start to cry. It's getting lighter outside – there's only one curtain in the whole flat, and even that's just a moth-eaten old sheet chucked over the curtain rail. Most people have fallen asleep, but the music's still playing really loudly, so Will storms over and smashes the off button so hard the stereo nearly falls off the sideboard. We go into the kitchen. One of the girls is naked, passed out on the lino. I go back into the lounge and take the sheet off the curtain pole and throw it over her. I find a jumper and roll it up and put it under her head. I can hear someone throwing up in the bathroom. I don't think this was what God had in mind for Saturday nights. I can't see God getting off his face and puking up all over a stranger's toilet, then getting up in the morning and putting his best suit on and going to church. But then he wouldn't go to church, would he, because he's already God? Meanwhile, Will's found a big knife. It was stuck in the middle of a third of a birthday cake. "Perfect," he says, nodding approvingly, and he holds the blade out to me so I can grab it by the handle, which is kind – he could have cut himself.

And then I'm getting out of someone's car – it might have been a taxi – I kind of fall out of the back of the passenger side, and onto the kerb and the low strip of pavement between the road and the sliding automatic doors of the hospital entrance. Will grabs me round my middle and yanks me up into a standing run. Naturally, I head for the doors in front of me, but Will pulls me off to one side, and we end up running for ages, and I think we're heading away from the hospital and out into the residential streets, but then we suddenly run past a blue and white sign, and I catch site of the word I've been waiting to see for what seems like so long – The Beeches. He steers me away from the main drive I attempt to run down. "What the fuck?" I breathe, as the sign for reception disappears from view, and we fall together into a rhododendron bush.

"Right, sit here for five minutes and sort yourself out. Then go to reception, tell them you're her brother and ask if you can visit her," Will orders me, earnestly, pushing his new glasses up onto his head so he can wipe his eyes. His eyes are so bright and big. It's probably all the coke.

"Are you okay, Will? I can't make sense of this – I feel a bit weird. Maybe we should leave it for today …".

"No!" Will cuts me off adamantly. "If you sit around waiting for the perfect day, nothing will ever happen. If you love her and you know she's carrying your baby, you need to speak to her!" He reads the expression on my face, and briefly embraces me, then smooths my hair down close over my head, and pulls a bottle of water from somewhere, along with some painkillers and chewing gum. "Good luck," he says gravely, staring me in the face. "Don't let them take her from you. Most of them don't think about what they're doing, and the ones who do, don't care."

And then he's gone.

I sit in my hiding place deep in the rhododendron, and try to clear my head. I try to play back everything that has happened since I turned my back on The Stables; the smell of alcohol, the train, the man at the bar, the music, the spliff, the glasses, the girl I covered with a sheet – and there I stop. The girl with the sheet. I'd covered her with the sheet from a window? I did it because she had no clothes on, and I didn't want her to be cold, but had I covered her face over, too? The harder I try to remember the image of her on the floor as I'd turned away, the more uncertain I become. I think she'd been lying on her side, like she was asleep; but had she actually been on her back? She'd been really drunk – and the rest. I should have put her in the recovery position. I hadn't put her in the recovery position. But did I not do that because she was already dead? Is that why I'd thrown the sheet over her? Then all I can see are the bumps of her face and body under the sheet, and her bare feet sticking out of the end, waiting for someone to come and put a tag on them. I think I'm only seeing it in my head. I think I am. I'm shivering.

I wipe my hands on my jeans, and there's so much sweat the action actually leaves a mark. I look around, wildly, but for what? All I can see are the thick, dark leaves, and patches of grey tarmac in the small gaps between them.

What had Will said? He'd taken that knife out of the

birthday cake. I'd thought it had been all smeared with chocolate icing or buttercream or whatever, but had it been dark red? I open my shaking hands and examine the palms. There's reddish-brown on them, but it might just be dirt – when was the last time I washed? – and the soil is red in Devon; something to do with it having been underwater in the time of the dinosaurs and the salt water had made it rusty? I can't remember. I'm not sure about anything, other than the conversation I'd overheard, with Heather and Bonnie saying that Lizzie was probably at The Beeches with Dr Whittle's baby. But it isn't Dr Whittle's baby – it's my baby. I swig from the bottle of water, put a piece of gum in my mouth, and dribble some more water over my face and hands, and smooth it through my hair. I wipe the excess on my jeans. I clamber out of the bush, check there's no one around, and start walking down the path to reception. When I know I'm in sight of the people in the building, I open the bottle of water, make to swig the last of it, but trip, and make a bit of a show of getting water on my hands and jeans. As I approach the building, I try to catch my reflection in the windows. I look sketchy as fuck.

My heart's racing by the time I reach the automatic doors, so I do the breathing exercises I've learnt in therapy, in an attempt to calm myself. I keep shaking. I've got to the doors too quickly and have to wait while they register my presence, and slowly but noisily open. And then it's like someone's chucked a load of ice down my back and down my throat at the same time. An image flashes through my mind. It's Will's hand passing me the knife by the handle, while he holds the gooey blade. I know I don't have it on me, but I pat my pockets and feel round the top of my jeans anyway. What the hell have I done with it?!

Sasha

Well. This is an insight. And the name of the club is so fitting it's almost laughable. Underground, with a low, red ceiling and candles forced into empty wine bottles illuminating the few tables. It's full to capacity, and in order to breath properly, you have to stand as close as you are able to the entrance, where the door is wedged open. The clientele is predominantly adolescent, with a few ageing rockers whose ridiculous tattoos have faded to green. It wouldn't surprise me if Erazmus struts in – I've seen him, in his car, Led Zeppelin blaring from the open windows. I've seen him, with that patient of his, Elizabeth Rowe, in his car, laughing, listening to music in the car park by the railway station in Tamehaven, thinking that no one will notice them. I've seen him kiss her. I only wish I'd had a camera with me – there's no arguing with photographic evidence. How dare he be getting his kicks, while I throw flowers for Amber into the sea. I will destroy that man.

I tell them my name is Liam. I've had a 'toke on a spliff', I've had tequila; I push my way to the front of the sticky, dripping bar and order a cider in a plastic – I almost said 'glass'! – receptacle, just to immerse myself in the experience. Being unable to find a vacant table, I make my way back to the entrance of the club, the cider slopping over the sides of the plastic tumbler as I go, to breathe some fresh air, more than anything, but people continue flooding in, so I walk towards the – dance floor? – where people are jumping about to the music. There's a small space at the back, by the sound crew, so I take it, placing my cider onto the top of an amplifier which bears the legend, 'This is not a beer table'. The band are loud, but actually very good. I find myself

174

watching them intently. The lead singer is spectacularly good on the guitar, and the piano. I move a little to one side, to see if he is reading music. He isn't. The music is in his blood, like it had been in Amber's. She should have been here, enjoying this band. My rage at the injustice consumes me once again, and I unconsciously squeeze the plastic tumbler. The golden liquid is forced over the edge, and it runs down my hand and splashes onto the floor and onto my shoes. In anger, I drain what's left in it, and dash it onto the filthy, wet floor. The tall, thin lad I'd seen on the steps staggers past and treads on it. It splits down the middle, and in that instant, I realise who he is. He's that new patient of Erazmus' – Dominic Whiley. I've read his file. It's extensive. He has schizophrenia. He's supposed to be confined to the grounds of The Stables.

In spite of my insobriety, I am instinctively inclined to find a phone box, call the care home and inform the staff, but I am unable do that without leaving him unsupervised. I decide to shadow him, and make the call when the opportunity arises.

He lurches over to the far wall, props himself up against it, and is engrossed in the band's performance. He doesn't have a drink. There are a few drinks waiting for their owners' return, on the amplifier that is not a beer table, one of which is an unopened bottle of water. I grab it, and wait. Dominic keeps running his hands through his hair, and repositioning himself against the damp, red wall. I make my way over to him, lightly touch his shoulder with my hand, and say in my best working-class accent, "Are you all right, mate? It looks like you could do with some of this," and I offer him the bottle. He smiles weakly, thanks me, takes and drains half of it.

"Thanks, mate," he repeats. "I feel a bit sketchy."

Dominic proves to be an intelligent and entertaining companion. I am duty bound to guide him through the evening and ensure he returns to The Stables safely – I will not let Dr Whittle's incompetence fail this young man. After a while, we sit with our backs against the wall, and allow the bass to reverberate up the soles of our feet and our spines, and when the band finish their set with an almighty crash of drums and guitars, we both get to our feet and cheer with everyone else. The blue-haired pianist springs into the air, his guitar slung round his back, snatches up the microphone and simply says, "Ta!" before whipping his guitar over his head and off his shoulder and, along with the curly-haired bassist, and the other guitarist who is mainly piercings, stabs his instrument into the bass drum.

The drummer leaps up, runs to the front of the stage, and slaps them on their backs. They are all laughing. I cannot comprehend how the drummer has managed to perform like that after smoking so much marijuana. He tosses his drumsticks into the crowd, picking out Dominic and, by default, myself, grins and beckons us over.

The 'backstage' area is a dark, concrete-walled square illuminated by a single bare light bulb, off a corridor behind a curtain. We follow the band inside, and everyone flops down on the battered leather sofa and the beanbags that are scattered around the space. The blond lad who had offered me the spliff when I arrived at the club – who transpired to be the drummer – produces a bottle of tequila and declares that his 'mate' will be along soon with some more 'gear'.

And when that mate arrives – another tall, thin man with dyed red hair, who produces a handful of 'baggies' out from his boots – Dominic lurches to his feet, and shouts, "Will!"

The thin drug dealer whips round to face him, and hisses, "Dom! What the hell are you doing here?! Aren't you supposed to be …"

Dominic cuts him off with a flash of his eyes. Will is evidently concerned, and as I attempt to piece together the connection between them, the blue-haired singer, says, "No way, man! Are you two twins or something?!"

"Brothers," Will affirms, with a tight smile.

"Ah, so *this* is the guy who 'fucked up' your life!" the drummer, James, laughs, punching Will on the arm. Dominic doesn't seem to have noticed – he's shaking his head, and I wonder if he's hearing voices. Will glares at James, then switches his stare to me, silently demanding to know who I am, so I smile warmly and say, "I'm Liam. Want a shot?"

With a glance at his brother, Will pulls the nearest beanbag over and sits down next to Dominic. We all take a shot – I am compelled to for the sake of appearances – pass around another spliff, and eventually the singer yells, "All back to mine!" and everyone struggles to their feet, and trudges out of the club, up the cold, metal steps, and back out into the blessed fresh air of Victoria Street. There are still a few inebriated stragglers wandering about. We weave through the damp streets of Exeter, through a churchyard, where several of our party find it amusing to lie above the dead with their heads against the tombstones, smoking spliffs. I think of Amber, and feel a sobering rush of hatred. Finally, we arrive at a once beautiful Victorian house that is now bedsits, and someone opens the door.

Laughing – for differing reasons – we all make our way up narrow stairs to the singer's flat. I am disinclined to touch the dirty banister, but my balance has gone, and I am extremely tired, so I grab it, and haul myself up. Dominic attempts to do likewise, but his hand grasps nothing but air, and he stumbles on the stairs, steadying himself with his other hand on the pileless, cheap, blue carpet. I support him, and guide his hand to the banister, laughing, and calling him a "pisshead-stoner". Apparently, this is a term of endearment.

The flat is essentially a drugs den. Some girls appear, and are dancing. One of the lads orders them to strip. I leave the main room and find the bathroom. After relieving myself, I splash water over my wrists and face, and rinse my mouth. I'm tired, and I still haven't made the call – we'd passed a phone box but I hadn't dared to stop in case I lost them. I wonder how I can get Dominic – and myself – out of this situation. Drying myself with a burgundy hand towel which does not smell clean, I decide to stay for five minutes and ensure that Dominic is occupied, then slip out to the phone box. I can pretend I've gone to call my own dealer. It appears that everyone will be crashing here for the night.

As I exit the bathroom, habitually pulling the door closed behind me and almost pulling the tarnished brass doorknob out of its hole in the process, I hear Dominic and his brother having a heated conversation in hushed tones, in the kitchen. I stay stock-still, listen, and watch in horror as Will passes Dominic a knife. He holds it by the blade, so Dominic has to take the handle. I cough loudly, and bang the bathroom door shut, before walking into the kitchen, where I ask the brothers if they'd like a coffee. While the grubby plastic kettle boils, I break off a chunk of the chocolate cake from which Will has pulled the knife – I presume Dominic has hidden it under his T-shirt – and stuff it into my mouth with what I hope is a grin. I follow them into the main room, and we flop onto the leather sofa.

The smash of glass wakes me. I am lying on the sofa, with a splitting headache, and an awful taste in my mouth. Then I remember, sit up quickly and survey the room. The dark shape of Will is disappearing down the stairs; Dominic is scuffing broken glass into a pile, while scrabbling with a sheet. The orange glow from the streetlight right outside the house illuminates the room, and I realise the sheet had been the makeshift curtain. Dominic throws the sheet over a naked girl, then hurries off to catch up with his brother. I scramble up, softly descend the stairs, wait until Dominic and his brother are a safe distance away, then retrace our route through the churchyard, walking as quickly as I have ever walked, to the public phone booth. I ought to call the police, but in doing that, will I condemn Dominic to a life incarcerated? Deciding to phone The Beeches, I heave open the heavy door. The stench of urine hits me. The handset has been wrenched from its cord. With a growl, I sprint in the direction of the college. I'd been fuming the previous evening when I had been unable to find a space in any of the university car parks, and had been forced to leave my car on the side of the road by the college, but I now I am intensely glad. I open the boot and remove the overnight bag I keep in there. Being so very early in the morning, there is no one around. I have to make myself presentable as quickly as I can. If nothing happens, at least I'll be in good time for my meeting. I climb into the back of my car.

After a perfunctory rub down with wet wipes, I comb my hair, spray myself liberally with antiperspirant, and don a clean shirt. I take two ibuprofen with half a bottle of Evian and – although I find it vulgar in the extreme – I put three sticks of Orbit gum into my mouth and chew. Then I get into the driver's seat, start the ignition, and head directly to The Beeches.

I pull up by the side of the road near the entrance sign for the psychiatric unit, and exit my car. There is litter on the pavement – cigarette butts, an empty plastic bottle that once contained cheap cider, the remains of a kebab, and a splat of vomit. I shake my head in disgust, and something catches my eye. It's a train ticket, and lying next to it is a NUS card belonging to a student named Nicholas Evans. Nicholas Evans. He wrote *The Horse Whisperer*; which had been Amber's favourite novel. I have a copy at home. I am torn. I have a chance to avenge my sister and bring down Erazmus Whittle; I have a duty of care to Dominic. I sob. In every war there is collateral damage. I take the card, and return to my vehicle.

Expecting to have a long wait before Dominic and Will arrive, I switch the engine off completely, a little annoyed that I now won't be able to listen to music, but I don't want the battery to die. I lean back in my seat, determined to stay awake, but I'm exhausted; that cake had been laced with something, and I cannot keep my eyes open any longer.

The familiar nagging of my bladder wakes me, and I curse myself for drifting off. I scan the area. People are passing by; cars are coming and going. About twenty minutes have passed. There is no sign of Dominic or Will, but I don't believe I've missed them. They would have had to walk to the bus station to catch the H bus to the hospital, before making their way to The Beeches. I doubt very much that they even know how to get to it. I allow myself a smile, but the need to urinate is now pressing, and I consider using the facilities in The Beeches, but as I don't want to miss the brothers' arrival by going inside, there is nothing I can do except hide in one of the thick rhododendron bushes that surround the unit, and relieve myself there. I do not take the decision lightly. I have been utterly out of my comfort zone for the last twenty-four hours, and all I want is to purify myself with a long, scalding shower, and a litre of bottled water. I will throw away the clothes I am wearing, maybe even get some new glasses.

I'm startled by a cry from the street. I zip up my trousers and hastily disentangle myself from the bushes. As I do so, I hear the automatic doors of the unit clunk open. I freeze.

"LIARS! You're all a bunch of fucking LIARS!" It's Dominic. He has his back to me, and is shouting at the reception area of the unit. My view is obstructed by the dark, fleshy leaves of the rhododendron, but I can make out shadows of the staff moving behind their protective glass. Then Dominic becomes aware of the noise from the street, which is escalating – cries are becoming screams. As he turns towards the awful sound, I duck further back into the bushes, and let him run past me, and off the hospital grounds. When he's out of sight, I sprint in his direction.

Dominic is standing, frozen, staring at the carnage. There are people writhing on the floor, but I have to do what I'm about to do, for Amber. "Dominic, it's me, Liam," I tell him redundantly, holding his distorted face until he looks me in the eyes. He nods, and I push him to my car, shove him in the back, and order him to stay there. He nods, tears streaming down his cheeks, and I lock the car and race to the nearest prone person. There is a lot of blood, and there are two more casualties – one is screaming, the other silent and motionless. Removing my shirt, I thrust it over the gushing wound in the woman's shoulder, tell her I am getting help, and to apply pressure, and dash over to a woman who is writhing and screaming. As I do so, I witness a tall man running away. It looks very much like Dominic, but that can't be, because Dominic is secured in my car. As he rounds the corner, the running man's hair slips. It's a wig. Without breaking his stride, he tugs it back onto his head. The hair underneath is red.

Erazmus

The male officer's radio crackles, and he stands and walks out of the family room to take the call. The blonde police officer smiles at me, and I haul myself up in frustration, and run my hands through my hair. I can see the male officer outside, talking to his colleagues; I also see nurses and doctors running past. I turn to the female officer, and am about to ask what's going on, when my pager beeps.

I read the message and exit the room, making eye contact with the sergeant, who nods at me; then I turn and run after the medical staff.

Dawn is breaking as I arrive outside the house I once shared with Julia. I turn straight onto the drive and all but dump the car. I've never understood what it truly feels like to be exhausted before. I ache all over, my stomach is growling but even the thought of food makes me nauseous, my mouth is dry and stale, and my head is simultaneously fuzzy and stabbing. Slamming the front door closed behind me, I drop everything I'm carrying at the bottom of the stairs and pull myself up using the banister. I walk straight into the bedroom and flop onto the bed. I thought sleep would come and give me some relief from this misery almost immediately, but it doesn't. I lie there, face down on the duvet, the square, frilled cushions which Julia insisted should cover most of the bed falling onto my face no matter how much I shove them away. I haven't bothered to draw the curtains, so the room grows lighter and lighter, and in the end, I give up.

I make my way to the kitchen, where I drink a pint of water, take ibuprofen and paracetamol, make a weak, milky coffee, and eat a Twix. Standing in my kitchen, forcing myself to chew the chocolate bar slowly, I look around. At some point in my life, I must have been proud of this kitchen, with its designer fitted units, its ice cube-dispensing fridge-freezer, its majestic solid wooden table. Majestic – that's the word that sprang to mind. Why had we bought such an enormous table, when there were just the two of us? I consider putting the house up for sale, fully furnished. What will another family make of this room? I see a wide-rimmed glass vase full of sweet peas and freesias in the kitchen window. I see a wooden fruit bowl in the centre of the table, overflowing with fresh apples, pears, bananas and peaches. I see a couple of cats curled up together in a patch of sunlight that has fallen across an open newspaper, and two border collies bouncing about, eager for their morning walk. I see three children, aged five, eight and ten noisily eating their breakfasts; Honey Nut Loops spilling from the cereal box as one of the girls tries to play the game on the back, the middle child whining from over the top of her *Each Peach Pear Plum* book that her little brother is pulling faces and throwing crayons at her. I see a crisp-suited man ruffle the hair of each of his children as he makes his way over to his soft, curvy, sleepy, smiling wife, who is making porridge on the stove, to take the mug of tea she holds out to him, and kiss her on the mouth. The scene plays out in my mind's eye, and reflected in the glass oven door, I see a tired, dishevelled middle-aged man standing alone in a pristine, soulless kitchen, drinking cold coffee and eating the last bar of chocolate in the fridge, while his career and his marriage crumble down around him.

I don't know how long I've sitting on the kitchen floor, my back against a cupboard, my head between my knees, but the painfully loud ring of the telephone startles me back to the moment.

"Hello?" I speak into the receiver and wince at the despondency in my voice.

"Erazmus? Erazmus, it's Faye. Faye Farefield? You know, your colleague and friend for over twenty years?!"

I can't help but smile. Her voice – more specifically its tone – warms me into optimism. I let myself return her greeting with a chuckle.

"I presume you haven't slept yet, but I felt it was my duty – as said friend and colleague – to update you as soon as I could." I hold my breath. Lizzie.

"Lizzie is all right." Relief consumes me, and I sob.

"Lizzie is all right," Faye reiterates. "The team in A and E said you saved her life with that defib. She's been moved to a private room on a different ward, and has a police officer on duty outside."

I'm about to cut Faye off with a torrent of questions, but she raises her voice and speaks over me.

"As far as I can make out, Julia has been charged with attempted murder." Faye pauses. "And so has Dominic Whiley."

I go completely cold and numb. Faye waits for me to speak. "W-w-what?!" is all I can muster.

"He stabbed three people, Erazmus – one of them in the neck. Sasha Grosvenor caught him at The Beeches. The police found the knife in the bushes – it had Dominic's prints all over it."

"Wait! What the hell was Sasha doing at The Beeches?"

"Erazmus! Did you hear me? Dominic has just tried to murder three complete strangers! What Sasha was doing at The Beeches is neither here nor there – I think he had a meeting or something – anyway, that's not all." She pauses, and I let the silence hang. "Lizzie wants to see you."

Lizzie

Erazmus picks me up from the hospital, and drives us straight to the seaside. He puts a Bluetones CD on in the car, because he says it's more uplifting than Radiohead. We end up laughing; two pale, thin people with bags under their eyes, dressed in black singing away to *Reservoir*. It's sunny, with little fluffy cirrus clouds in a forget-me-not sky. There's a gentle breeze, the tide at Tamehaven is far enough out for there to be a strip of sand to lie on, and the waves roll in and out like a lullaby. Erazmus buys us 99s, and we eat them while we saunter up to the end of the pier. Erazmus checks there is no one else around, and then slides his free arm around my waist. We stand at the furthest tip of the pier and look out to the horizon. I notice something yellow floating in the water.

"Is that a ...?" I ask Erazmus, pointing with the remains of my ice cream cone. He peers out over the softly rolling waves, and pulls his glasses further down his nose.

"I'm not sure," he replies, and something compels us to keep it watching it until it's pushed nearer. "It's a rose," he says, quietly, as we watch it bob around the legs of the pier.

"There's another one," I whisper. "And another." My eyes begin to water.

"Hmm," says Erazmus, turning me away. "Let's go."

I thought he meant back to his house in Eskwich, but Erazmus takes the coast road, and when we drop into Swansburne, he navigates the one-way system until we'd almost doubled back on ourselves, and turns left at the bus stop by the railway line into a street called Marine Parade. Cars are parked at an angle almost all the way to the cliffs and the tunnel, and he stops in the first vacant space. I thought we were going for a walk up to the big tree at the top of the cove round the corner, but he steers me towards the little B&B with the turrets.

"I've always wanted to stay here! How did you know?"

"I didn't. I just really like the place and I know the lady who runs it," he replies.

I'm delighted when Erazmus asks if we can stay in one of the turret rooms – even more pleased that one is available. The room itself is basic, but I immediately run over to the big windows and open them. The fresh, salty smell of the sea floods in like sunshine, and we stand there, arms around each other, looking out, listening to the waves and the rumble of the trains. Erazmus goes out to get us some food, and returns with fish and chips wrapped in paper, and a bottle of Cava. And then we make love, and fall asleep to the lull of the waves and the intermittent cries of gulls.

Sasha

It's a pyrrhic victory.

After the proverbial smoke clears, I resign my position at The Meadows, but I take up their offer of bereavement counselling; I also lodge a complaint against Dr Whittle about the events regarding the suicide of my sister. Julia Whittle has been diagnosed with post-traumatic stress disorder, and it has been accepted that in attempting to kill Elizabeth, she had suffered a psychotic episode. She has not gone to prison – she has been moved to a secure hospital, and to Erazmus' despair, this renders him incapable of divorcing her. In fact, stoic martyr that he is, he visits her daily, like a good husband. But I saw him with Elizabeth on the pier in Tamehaven, and followed them back to their love nest. I'd just left Amber some flowers and tears and a promise, but I had a camera with me this time. I took a series of photos, which I will post to the powers that be. His beloved career is over. But I am unable enjoy this.

Whatever higher force there is – if indeed there is one – has an evil streak. As do we all, I suppose. Whoever said that there were only two things you could be sure of in life – death and taxes – was wrong. There is a third: irony. Bitter, bitter irony.

I know that Dominic Whiley did not attack those people, and I am sure it was Will I witnessed running away. But there is no proof. Dominic is schizophrenic. He has auditory and, possibly, visual hallucinations too. He was in a state of emotional distress. He was high. He was inebriated. He had missed at least one dose of his medication. He cannot be sure what happened the evening he went to The Coal Mine. He admitted that he thinks he killed one of the drunken girls at the after-party – except no one died there that night. I did, however, read in the newspaper that one of the girls made an allegation of sexual assault, which she later withdrew. And Dominic's fingerprints were all over the handle of the knife. I said nothing to the police; to do so would have killed my career in its infancy. I am getting justice for Amber. Dominic is collateral damage. This way, Dr Whittle has failed another patient. He is an old man with old ideas and a narrow mind. This health service is crying out for new blood. I am that new blood. This is too important to risk telling the truth. I am doing the good work. I am the necessary change.

But I am imprisoned. I will have to hold this secret till my grave. I have caused a young man to believe that his illness is so bad that he harmed people. I have caused him to spend who knows how long in a secure psychiatric hospital. And if he dies as a result of this? Then I am little better than Erazmus. When I am not at work, I clean my home, and pray.

Epilogue

How can it be that the men I love hurt me so badly? Erazmus works. He tends to his wife. When he feels he can spare the time, we meet in the station car park. I refuse to enter his home – not that he has ever directly invited me back there. When we spend time together, it's in that little B&B by the sea. I am so much better now, he thinks, that he has suggested I get a voluntary job in a charity shop. He even joked that I could help the duck warden. I am not acute any more, he says. I have to get on with my life. But what can I do, really? There are no decent jobs in Devon, and even if there were, who would take on someone who's been sectioned? I thought about trying to get pregnant so Erazmus would stay with me, but that would just make more mess. I am out of options. Third time lucky.

I'm walking along the seafront in Tamehaven. There's a hell of a cold wind coming off the sea, and it's whipping up the waves. The tide is on its way in, too. I go to do what I've always done when I come to the beach, and throw a stone into the surf, for luck, but when I look at what I've picked up, it's a piece of green sea glass.

I throw it into the waves with the whole force of my body. It splashes into the water above the surf line, which is a really good throw, for me. I stand there, staring at the spot where it sank, and then I notice that there's something in the water. My eyes aren't great at distance, so I squint. Then I see what it is, and a chill runs through my body. It is a yellow rose.

And that is the moment when something changes in me. Roses don't just appear in the ocean, in the same place, regularly. I am under the pier now, and it's a grey day anyway, but under the boards, it's really dark. The sound of the sea echoes off the supporting posts and the curved sea wall. If I sat here for maybe half an hour, the sea would consume me, and no one would notice. There are a couple of people on the wet, red sand, walking their dogs, the hoods of their anoraks pulled up against the drizzle and the spray. They can't see me. I wouldn't have to do anything more than sit, wait, and hold my nerve. I imagine the thin trickle of wave that is pushed up the furthest, reaching the tip of my Converse boots. I imagine the first shock of the icy water as it soaks through the canvas; my feet becoming acclimatised to it, and I don't register the level rising. Then the salt water would begin to diffuse up my jeans, and then I would be sitting in it, my back still up against the concrete defending wall. I imagine the cold starting to take hold. I imagine by the time it is up to my waist, I will be shivering, and my feet would probably be floating. I wonder when I would begin to feel the pull. I wonder at what point I would be unable to remain sitting. I wonder if an innate response would kick in, and I'd start trying to swim. Maybe I would have hypothermia by then. The waves would be crashing up against the wall by this point; maybe crashing back over my head. Or maybe the tide would have sucked me out, and I'd be trying to scream and call for help, struggling against a riptide, the pier disappearing from view. Maybe I'd see the grey fin of a basking shark. Would I be terrified if I was that panicked and that cold? Maybe I'd see a dolphin. Maybe I would be saved by a pod of dolphins. Someone died here, I think.

And that's when I stand up. The waves are lapping against my shoes. I need to get off the beach now before it becomes submerged. My heart races, and I splash across the strip of sand that remains visible above the water. It is really cold, and my feet are numb before I reach the concrete steps up to the promenade. The sea is level with the top of the first step, and I scrabble up the steps in a panic, my hands sandy and wet, grasping the concrete. There are only ten steps, but when I reach the promenade, I am crying and shivering. I hadn't noticed, sitting as I was under the pier, that the drizzle had become heavy rain. There was no one around. I could have died. I could still die – I could jump back in. I am losing myself. I am at a crossroads – a real one, this time. I feel the urgency. I hold onto the metal barrier as tightly as I can with my wet, numb, hands, and I am suddenly reminded of clinging onto the barrier at the front of a gig watching that band with the funny name. I look at the sea, trying to remember the name, and I see a rose on the crest of a wave. It disappears from view as it smashes against the concave sea wall, and is gone for a few seconds. I wait, and see it bob to the surface before crashing and disappearing again. It loses its petals. I cannot watch any longer. Someone died here.

Turning my back on the ocean, I decide that I will not die here. Shaking with the cold, and probably shock, I make my way towards the station. I'll go back to the B&B in Swansburne and tell Erazmus that whatever kind of relationship we are having is over. He doesn't love me. I doubt he ever did. Then I'll get my stuff together and walk over to the phone box at the end of the road. I'll call my parents and ask them to come and pick me up, and while I'm waiting for them, I'll go to the library and see if they've got any leaflets about Exeter College. I think they do an art foundation course there. I let myself be warmed by hope, and am smiling by the time I reach the station.

But standing alone on gloomy platform two, I suddenly think of Lydia. Guilt flooding through me, I sprint back over the bridge, and jump on the train to Bishopsham. I have to do this first; I have to tell Heather what Dunstan has been doing. I can barely sit still in my seat, and although my gaze never strays from the tiny dead fly on the rubber window surround, I don't notice any of the scenery flashing behind it. I'm standing by the door before the train pulls into Bishopsham station, and walk as quickly as I can through the town and up the hill towards The Stables. I'm going to help my friend, finally. I smile again. Things are going to be okay.

I hear the sirens before I realise that I can smell smoke. By the time I'm halfway up the hill, my eyes are stinging and there's an acrid taste in my dry mouth. People are shouting. My heart thumps. There's a crowd of people out on the road, and there are police everywhere. Adrenalin makes my head fuzzy. Someone is shouting my name. Heather. She rushes up to me, arms spread wide to block my path. The police have formed a barrier and are pushing people back. The air is thick. Heather's face is etched with horror, her eyes dilated and wet. Her hands are on my shoulders. I can't say anything, because I already know.

"The Stables is on fire," she gasps, "and they can't find Dunstan or Lydia!"

Fantastic Books
Great Authors

darkstroke is
an imprint of
Crooked Cat Books

- Gripping Thrillers
- Cosy Mysteries
- Amazing Horrors
- Fascinating Historicals
- Exciting Fantasy
- Young Adult and Children's
  Adventures
- Non-Fiction

Discover us online
www.darkstroke.com

Find us on instagram:
www.instagram.com/darkstrokebooks

Printed in Great Britain
by Amazon